Cracked
Classics

# Crack open all the books in

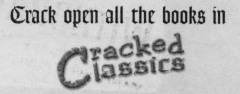

## Cracked Classics

# Romeo & Juliet

## Crushing on a Capulet

### By Tony Abbott

Hyperion
New York

Text copyright © 2003 by Tony Abbott
Cracked Classics, Volo, and the Volo colophon are trademarks of Disney Enterprises, Inc.
Cover illustrations by Gris Grimly

Printed in the United States of America
First Edition
1 3 5 7 9 10 8 6 4 2
This book is set in 11.5-pt. Cheltenham.

ISBN 0-7868-1329-6
Visit www.volobooks.com

# Chapter 1

"Ha, ha, ha!" I laughed as I stared at the door of Mr. Wexler's classroom.

"Hey, Devin, it's English class, not TV," said my best-pal-even-though-she's-a-girl, Frankie Lang, who just happened to walk up behind me. "What's with all the laughing?"

Chuckling still, I pointed to a small sign taped to the classroom door and said, "Behold!"

The sign read PLAY IN THE CAFETERIA TODAY.

I smiled. "Frankie, our teacher has given us an assignment. We must play in the cafeteria!"

She nodded. "Wow . . . but why—"

"Never question such things!" I said sternly. "When teachers tell you to play, you play! This alone is good. But when they tell you to play in the cafeteria, which is where they keep the food, then, Frankie, the stars shine down on us, destiny is on our side, and school is good."

"That was a beautiful speech, Devin," she said. "And let me be the first to say that I approve of this new subject of 'play.' In fact, I'm thinking we should be in honors. We'd be excellent."

"Then, let us go and excel," I said happily, heading with my friend to the cafeteria.

Now, at Palmdale Middle School, where Frankie and I are sixth graders, we have one of these cafeterias that is also the auditorium. It has a stage at one end, with a big maroon curtain, a flagpole, and everything. Frankie and I like to sit on the edge of the stage to eat. Until the lunch ladies see us and chase us off.

Just as I was planning what sort of game we'd play, we rounded the corner and entered the caf. Right away, I knew something was wrong. Instead of a lot of playing going on, there was a lot of what looked like work.

First of all, everyone from our English class was hustling around, pushing the lunch tables aside and setting up chairs. Some kids were actually sweeping the floor.

"How are we supposed to play with all this work going on?" I asked.

"Beats me," said Frankie.

"Ah! Frankie and Devin! You're here!" called a voice.

We turned to see our teacher Mr. Wexler next to

the stage, a small book in one hand, and a stack of weird, brightly colored clothes in the other.

"What's with the pile of pajamas?" Frankie asked.

"They're costumes," our teacher replied dryly.

"Costumes?" I said, stepping back. "It's not Halloween yet. Costumes for what?"

"For what, you ask?" He smiled largely, put the costumes down, handed the small book to Frankie, and using both hands, yanked open the curtain.

"Ta-da!" he chimed.

I gasped. On the stage were big wooden cutouts of crooked, old-style buildings. To the left were some pink-colored buildings, to the right were a bunch of blue ones. In between was a small open square with a fountain. Sticking up behind the buildings were several wobbly towers with banners hanging from them.

It looked like a scene from some old fairy tale.

Mr. Wexler took a deep breath, cleared his throat, then spoke loudly: "'Two households, both alike in dignity—in fair Verona, where we lay our scene—from ancient grudge, break to new mutiny. . . .'"

He stopped.

We stared.

Finally, I spoke. "Mr. Wexler, the last time I checked, you were an English teacher. But you're not talking English. You're talking some other language. A weird one!"

He laughed. "No, no, Devin, it is English. In fact—it's Shakespeare, William Shakespeare, one of England's greatest playwrights. He's the author of *Romeo and Juliet*, the play we're putting on for the other classes today. Didn't you see the sign on the classroom door?"

"That sign said 'play in the cafeteria today,'" I said. "It means we're supposed to play in the cafeteria."

He shook his head. "No, it means we're *putting on* a play in the cafeteria!"

"Then the sign wasn't written in good English," I said.

"Neither is this," said Frankie, turning the book every which way. "The words are all crazy."

Our teacher chuckled. "True, Frankie, the language is different. After all, the play was written over four hundred years ago. But you'll see how the story comes alive when we perform it for the school on this stage today. These are some of the costumes our class will be wearing."

He held up the pajamas again.

I frowned. "Mr. Wexler, you must be speaking that other language again, because it sounded like you said our class will be wearing funny clothes on stage—"

"Exactly," said Mr. Wexler. "We've been reading *Romeo and Juliet* for the last week. So we're all quite familiar with the parts . . . wait . . . don't tell me you haven't read the play?"

4

I turned to Frankie. She turned to me.

Reading. That was the problem. As good as Frankie and I were at the playing thing, we weren't all that good at the reading thing. I've given this a lot of thought, and I think it has something to do with all the words they put in books. To get what's going on, you're supposed to read all of them. That's the problem.

"Um . . . define *read* . . ." said Frankie.

Mr. Wexler gave out a big sigh. "Yes, yes, I can just imagine. You were probably too busy playing around to read the book I assigned."

"Hey," I said, "it's what we're good at."

He made a face. "Well, in a nutshell, Romeo and Juliet are two young Italian people who fall in love—"

"Love?" I gasped. "Whoa! I thought school was supposed to be rated PG!"

Mr. Wexler laughed. "Oh, it's a wonderful play, full of romance, of course, but full of action, too. It ends rather badly, of course. It's one of Shakespeare's tragedies."

"It sounds pretty tragic," I mumbled to Frankie.

Mr. Wexler pointed to a building on the stage that had an upstairs balcony overlooking a garden filled with painted bushes. "The balcony scene between Romeo and Juliet is one of the most famous scenes ever. Why, just listen to this wonderful poetry. . . ."

He gazed up at the balcony, extended his hand

toward it, and launched into some pretty strange wordage.

"'But soft,'" he muttered, "'what light through yonder window breaks? It is the east, and Juliet is the sun—'"

All of a sudden, someone came out onto the balcony. We gasped. It was a woman, but not a young Italian woman, if you know what I mean. She had grayish hair pulled up tight behind her head, and wore a bright flowery dress.

"Mrs. Figglehopper!" Frankie said.

It *was* Mrs. Figglehopper, our school librarian.

She looked down at Mr. Wexler, clasped her hands together, then spoke some wacky lines of her own.

"'How camest thou hither, tell me? The orchard walls are high and hard to climb, and the place death, considering who thou art, if any of my kinsmen find thee here.'"

"'With love's light wings did I over-perch these walls,'" Mr. Wexler replied. "'For stony limits cannot hold love out, and what love can do, *that* dares love attempt. Therefore thy kinsmen are no stop to me. . . .'"

Let me tell you, it was very weird watching our teacher and our librarian talk like that. I was pretty embarrassed for them, although they didn't seem to be.

"Four hundred years old," Frankie grumbled, still

squinting at the book. "I guess people had more time on their hands back then. They needed it to figure out what the other people were saying!"

Mrs. Figglehopper tramped down the stairs from the balcony and came out on stage, full of chuckles.

"It's not that hard to understand!" she boomed. "Besides, a good story is a good story!"

"Quite right," added Mr. Wexler. "In fact, Mrs. Figglehopper and I shall be in today's play, too. Of course, not as Romeo and Juliet . . . oh, you know, I just had an idea. . . ."

He got a sudden weird look in his eye, and he moved that look over at me. "You know, Devin . . ."

"Uh-oh," I said, backing away. "Here it comes."

"Devin, performing in this play is the best way to learn it. If you want to do your best on our *Romeo and Juliet* test next week, you should probably play the part of Romeo. . . ."

I looked at my teacher. "I'm suddenly feeling faint. And I always faint at home. I'd better go there now—"

He blocked my way.

"And Frankie shall be Juliet!" said Mrs. Figglehopper, clasping her hands together again in delight.

Frankie gave the lady a gigantic frown. "Take that back, Mrs. F!" she said. "It's not even funny!"

"Actually, even though it's a tragedy, parts of

7

*Romeo and Juliet* are quite funny," said Mr. Wexler. "But, you'll enjoy the whole thing more when you are both speaking your speeches on that stage."

Frankie and I stared at each other, speechless.

"Good. It's settled," said Mrs. Figglehopper. "The PTA mothers have made costumes especially for your two roles. They're in the library workroom. Would you toddle off and bring them here? Thank you."

I was rooted to the floor in a kind of shock, still mumbling, "Me . . . play . . . on stage . . . lines . . . reading . . ."

Frankie was making a soft, whimpering sound. "Can't do this . . . can't do this . . . no, no, can't do this . . ."

But the two grown-ups had no sympathy. They were cruel. They were heartless. And to make us move faster, they began talking wacky again.

"'Arise, fair sun,'" said Mr. Wexler, "'and kill the envious moon, who is already sick and pale with grief—'"

"Me, too," I groaned. "Me, too."

But my lament did no good.

Frankie and I had no choice but to stumble off sadly to the library.

8

# Chapter 2

"Frankie, no way am I dressing up, PTA moms or no PTA moms," I said, as we made our way down the hall to the library. "Dressing up includes the word 'dress.' And I don't wear dresses!"

"Neither do I much," she said, squinting at the book again. "But you gotta take a look at this stuff. The lines don't even reach to the edge of the page."

I peered at the pages. "Already, I have a headache. What do you even call that stuff?"

"Poetry, I think," she said.

"Nuh-uh. Poetry is like 'Roses are red, violets are blue, I like peanut butter, you like glue.' This stuff is way too hard to understand. I predict we'll flunk this play. Imagine me, failing play. Talk about tragedy!"

Frankie chuckled. "But you know, Devin, we've sort of been in this situation before. Faced with reading a classic old book and getting A's on it anyhow."

"Don't go there," I said, shivering.

But, of course I knew what she meant.

The zapper gates.

We pushed open the main library doors, took a sharp right, and entered the library workroom.

Frankie and I knew the place pretty well. It was a small room with tables pushed up against two walls. We saw a bunch of funny costumes on one table. On the other were stacks of old dusty books needing repair. There was a copy machine, a computer, a scanner, and a printer. And in the middle of the room were bookshelves with hundreds of old classic books that Mrs. Figglehopper was repairing.

But the most important—and crazy—things in the room were the zapper gates. That was what Mrs. Figglehopper called an old set of security gates that she stored in the library workroom.

I was staring at them now. They actually looked like a doorway, except that the sides only went up partway, and there was no top.

Frankie and I knew all about them. They're the kind of gates that are supposed to go all *zzzt-zzzt!* when a book goes through them that hasn't been checked out the right way.

But these gates don't go all *zzzt-zzzt!*

They go *kkkk-kkkk!* And lightning flashes and thick, blue smoke fills the room and the wall behind the zapper gates cracks right open and you're sucked into a book.

That's right! Into a book!

It's happened to Frankie and me a few times already! And each time it's more incredible than the time before. We get all jumbled and tumbled around, then we get thrown out smack dab at the beginning of some old classic story—right there with the story's real characters.

It is very weird and very impossible.

But being impossible doesn't mean it's not possible!

Okay, maybe it does. But it happens anyway!

"I can't even read this!" said Frankie, shutting the book. "It's like somebody is punishing my brain—but my brain didn't do anything wrong!"

I laughed. "For sure. It usually doesn't do anything at all—hey, look!"

Right next to the pile of funny costumes was a box full of T-shirts. The shirts had pictures of this old dude on the front, and they said SHAKESPEARE under the picture. "What are these? Prizes if we're in the play?"

I pulled one on over my shirt. So did Frankie.

"Maybe if I could wear this, I might do a walk-on."

She chuckled. "You'd have to walk on in tights," she said, digging in the costume pile and holding up a pair of blue tights that were part of the Romeo outfit.

I stared at the wiggly things.

"Okay, this is where I check out. No way ever does Devin Bundy wear tights!" I started for the door.

"There's also swords," she said, holding up two bendy plastic toy swords that were next to the pile.

I stopped. "Swords? Mr. Wexler did say there was action in the play. And I like action toys." I flashed one of the swords around in the air. "Okay, then. I choose to be a swashbuckling old-time dude. On guard, Miss Frankie of Lang!"

She grabbed the other sword and grinned. "Same to you, Sir Devin of Bundy!"

We started clacking our weapons all around the room, leaping up to the tabletops and waving our swords at each other.

"Now, this is the sort of play I can get into!" I said.

It was fun. But fun has a way of not lasting too long.

On a really great leap from the book table to Mrs. Figglehopper's swivel chair, I accidentally lost my balance, fell back to the desk, and kicked the old *Romeo and Juliet* book clear across the room.

Yep, you guessed it. Right between the zapper gates.

*Kkkkk!*

The room exploded with bright blue light. The air shook, the floor quaked, Frankie and I tumbled to the floor, and the wall behind the gates cracked right open.

Instantly, thick, blue smoke poured from the crack.

"Oh, no!" I cried. "It's happening!"

Before we could make a move—*floop!*—the book was gone. Vanished. Disappeared into the swirling, dark smoke of the cracked wall.

The next instant—*floop! floop! floop!*—the costumes were gone, wiggly tights and all.

"Did what just happened really happen?" I said.

"I think so. The PTA moms will be very mad."

The library doors suddenly creaked open. Someone was coming toward the workroom.

"Frankie—we've got to get those costumes back!"

"And that book!"

"And we'd better do it right now!"

An instant later, Frankie and I were gone, too—*floop! floop!*—straight through the zapper gates and into the dark, swirling, smoky crack in the wall.

"Yikes!" cried Frankie.

"Yikes and a half!" I added.

Over and over we rolled. There were lots of legs and arms and costumes and props. It was like Frankie and I were inside some sort of classic-book clothes dryer, tumbling around and around until we were dumped down into a street in the pile of costumes.

I rolled over and over until I splatted against something flat and cold. Frankie slammed up against me. We both groaned for a while before we moved. When we got to our feet, we saw that all around us were old stone buildings and twisty streets. Some buildings were pink and some were blue.

In the center was an open square and a big stone fountain. But instead of spouting painted water, this one spouted actually real water.

"Frankie?" I said. "Do you see anything weird?"

"Devin, I don't see anything *not* weird!"

"What I mean is, this looks a lot like the stage set in the cafeteria, only it's really real. I think that's weird."

"Weird times two." Frankie picked the book up from the ground and opened it to the first page. "Okay, look, first things first. The setting of the story. Mr. Wexler said Romeo and Juliet were Italian, right? Well, it says it right here, just like he told us, 'In fair Verona where we lay our scene.' So I guess we're in Verona, Italy."

"Isn't Italy where all the meatballs are?"

She laughed. "With us here, there's at least two."

"Better make that four," I said, pointing to the far

14

side of the square. "Because here come a couple of guys wearing tights—"

Two men rushed into the square.

"They're wearing swords, too," said Frankie.

Spotting us instantly, the two tights-wearing men pulled out their deadly-looking swords and started running toward us, shouting something like "Get them!"

I turned to Frankie. "Can I just say something?"

"If you say it quick," she said.

"It's just one word," I said. "HIDE!"

# Chapter 3

But we couldn't hide. The two swordy guys were all over us like sauce on meatballs, carving shapes in the air with their swords and backing us all the way up against the bubbly, spurting fountain.

"Whoa, dudes!" I shouted. "Put away the pointy things! This is the land of macaroni, not shish kebab!"

"Silence, you, you—*Montague!*" snarled one of the men, drawing shapes around my head with his sword. "Draw your blade and fight us!"

"It's plastic!" I said, showing him how the toy sword bent every which way. "Besides, I'm not this Monty Glue you're looking for. I'm Devin Bundy—"

"And I'm Frankie Lang," said Frankie. "We're—"

"You're Montague spies, that's who you are!" said

the second man, his sword twitching an inch from our nostrils. "And we'll get you!"

"No, you won't!" shouted a loud voice from the far end of the square. We turned to see two new guys rush into the square, yanking out their pointy swords, too.

"If there are any spies to get," one of these new guys said, "*we* shall get them, you—Capulets!"

Our two men gasped. "You—Montagues! Get them!"

In a flash—*clang! clonk! pling!*—everybody was getting everybody else. The air rang with the sound of blade against blade. I mean, the four guys went at it like actors in some ancient sword-fighting movie.

I looked at Frankie. "I'd like to repeat what I said before."

"You said a lot of things."

"True, but the one particular thing I want to repeat is—HIDE!"

Without another word, Frankie and I dove under a cart standing in the square, and pulled the pile of genuine PTA mom costumes in front of us.

"Look, Frankie," I said, my head draped in something pink and silky. "I'm not following what's going on too well—"

"Sort of like in class, huh?"

"Sort of," I admitted. "But I'm thinking maybe

17

these Montague and Capulet guys are sort of like ene-mies."

"You think?"

"If I have to," I said. "And I think they're having a whopper of a family feud. With us in the middle."

"Not a good position to be in," she said as one of the Capulets fell back onto the cart, rolled off, thud-ded to the ground, jumped up, and leaped back into the fight.

"Look, Dev," she said, "I know you're not going to like it, but maybe the only way to stay alive here is to blend in. You know . . . get into costume?"

"Ha!" I blurted out, still with the silky thing on my melon. "Frankie, I can tell you right now. There is *no way* I am going to wear tights! I don't do dress up—"

*Clang!* One of the guys slammed his sword down on the cart and nearly sliced it—and us—in two.

"Okay, okay!" I cried. "I think I get the point—*his* point. But, if you tell anyone—ANYONE!—that I wore tights in this story, I will personally go on the PA and tell everyone that you still sleep with your teddy bear!"

"I sleep with two teddy bears, and it's a deal!" she said, tossing me a tunic—it was blue with a gray col-lar and silver buttons. I pulled it on over my Shakespeare T-shirt, then fished around in the tangle of costumes and found the pair of—ugh!—blue tights. I tugged them up my legs.

They felt *soooo* weird, I can't even describe it.

But, hey, at least they matched my top.

Frankie's outfit was a way-too-long purple gown with a funny headdress thingy that looked like a tangled butterfly net with tiny pillows on each side.

"I feel like a princess," she said.

*Fwish!* One of the men swung his sword all around and nearly sliced both pillows off Frankie's hat.

With blades clanging and swishing all around us, we crawled out from under the cart just in time to see yet another bunch of guys jumping into the fight.

"Pull yourselves apart, you fools, there are children here!" shouted one of the new guys, leaping into the scuffle, and moving us gently out of the way. He had a friendly face and a nice green tunic with gold buttons. "Put up your swords. You know not what you—"

Unfortunately, another man rushed up and tried to stop him from stopping the fight. I didn't like the look of this new character. First of all, he wore a black outfit, which meant he was probably nasty. Plus, he had slicked-back hair, which meant he was mean. If that wasn't enough, his eyes were close together and slitty, and he carried a sword with a jeweled handle.

All in all, he gave Frankie and me the shivers.

"So! Benvolio!" the slick-hair guy sneered at our nice green-suit guy. "Draw your sword and fight me."

"No, Tybalt," Benvolio said. "I seek to keep the peace. Put up thy Capulet sword, or use it to help me part these fighting men—"

"Peace?" snarled Tybalt. "I hate the word. As I hate all Montagues, and thee. Draw thy sword, coward!"

The argument was filled with thees and thys, but I sort of understood them.

"Hey, Frankie," I said. "It's almost as if this Shakespeare guy really *is* writing English! Old-style English, maybe, but I'm getting most of it."

"I'm getting it, too," she said. "Maybe because we're wearing costumes. We're sort of part of the play now."

"And if we have to choose sides," I said, "I like Benvolio."

"He seems like a good guy," she said.

Well, the clanging and clashing noise of the fight was so loud that it brought even more people into the square, including two older men who looked as if they had just woken up.

"Montague is the cause of this fight—where is he?" shouted one of the old men, pulling his shirt on with one hand and flashing his sword with the other.

"You old Capulet! I'll fight you right here!" growled a second old guy, dragging his own sword behind him.

"Whoa, get the respirators!" said Frankie, barely stifling a chuckle. "These two guys couldn't fight their way out of a tissue box!"

Just as the two geezers were set to go at it, a horn sounded. Everyone in the square froze as if they were playing freeze tag.

We heard the thundering of horses' hooves on the cobblestones, and an instant later, a guy dressed in a long shiny cape came riding into the street. He was followed by a bunch of soldiers with extra-big weapons.

"Who do you suppose he is?" I whispered.

"That is the Prince of Verona," Benvolio whispered out of the corner of his mouth. "Now, we are in trouble."

The prince jumped down from his horse and stared at the two old men. "Montague and Capulet!" he boomed. "Rebellious subjects! Enemies to the peace!"

The two old dudes hung their heads.

"Three times your warring families have disturbed the quiet of our streets!" the prince said.

"So, they've been at it for a while?" said Frankie.

"For years," whispered Benvolio.

"Know this!" the prince said. "If *ever* you disrupt our streets again, your lives shall pay the price. On pain of death, all men depart!"

Then he snapped his fingers, and his huge guards, who toted bigger swords than everyone else, separated the Montagues and the Capulets and made everyone leave the square.

"Where to now?" I whispered to Frankie as we blended into the crowd. "If this is like most stories, the people in the title are the main characters. Well, so far, we've seen Benvolio, Tybalt, old man Montague and similar old man Capulet, plus the prince, but no *Romeo*—"

"You there, you there—did you say Romeo?"

We turned to see old Mr. and Mrs. Montague hobbling over to us.

"I am Romeo's mother," the woman said. "Saw you him today?"

Frankie had the book open. She looked up and shrugged. "Um, we aren't exactly sure," she said. "What does he look like—"

Benvolio gave a little smile. "So early walking did I see your son. Towards him I made, but he stole into the wood."

The prince's guards finished herding all the Montague people into a side street off the square, then left.

"Benvolio," said Mr. Montague, putting his hand on the guy's shoulder. "As his friend, can you find our Romeo, and discover what is bothering him?"

"And can we come with you?" I asked.

Benvolio smiled. "Certainly. I will find him—"

Suddenly, there was a deep sighing sound, coming from around the next corner. "Oh, woe! Ay me!"

Benvolio chuckled. "Ha! I'd know that sigh anywhere. It's our very own Romeo. Step aside, my dear Lord and Lady Montague. My friends and I will discover what ails him."

I turned to Frankie. "Did you hear that? We're Benvolio's friends!"

"I heard," said Frankie, tucking the book into a pocket in her dress. "I think we have to pay attention. This play moves fast."

As Mr. and Mrs. Montague slipped away down the passage, we hustled around the corner after Benvolio.

There we saw a young man zigzagging down the street as if he didn't know where he was. He wore the usual stylish tights-and-tunic outfit, had brown hair, which badly needed a comb, and was sighing all over the place, practically fogging up the air. "Oh . . . oh!"

"That's Romeo?" said Frankie, her eyes going slightly buggy. "Oh, he's cute! He could have his own show!"

"Somebody gag me please," I coughed.

I would have started to choke myself, but I wasn't sure if anybody would stop me, so I didn't.

Romeo wandered closer, his eyes gazing up at the sky, barely managing to put one shoe in front of the other. He stopped every few feet to sigh loudly, slump his shoulders, roll his eyes, shake his head, stagger a foot or two more, then sigh all over again.

"He looks like he's just been told he has to go to summer school," I said. "What's his problem?"

"Is he sick?" asked Frankie.

"Sick in love, it seems to me," said Benvolio, a little smile on his lips. "But let's find out. Ho, there, Romeo!"

Romeo put his hand to his forehead, sighed again, lowered his eyes to us, brushed some dust from his tunic, then said, "This is not Romeo; he's some other where. He is with the one I love . . ."

"Tell us, then, cousin," said Benvolio, nudging us. "Who is it you love?"

Romeo sighed. "I love . . . a woman."

I laughed. "We pretty much guessed that. And I think I know what her name is. It's Jul—"

"Rosaline!" said Romeo. "My true love's name is Rosaline!"

Frankie and I looked at each other. "Uh-oh," I said. "Did we crash-land in the wrong play? Are we in *Romeo and Rosaline* by mistake?"

Frankie squinted at the pages of the book. "You know what I think? Romeo and Juliet haven't met yet."

"Sure, sure, I can see it all now," I said. "If they don't meet up, everybody will blame us for wrecking Shakespeare. Hey, Romeo, just so you know, we're Devin and Frankie. Friends of Benvolio. Nice to meet you."

Romeo barely looked at us. "Nice? Nice? My true love Rosaline is nice. Her hair is the color of the raven's wing, so black and long, her cheeks are like the whitest cream, and her eyes shine like pools. Rosaline is so rich in beauty, if you saw her eyes . . ."

Blah, blah, blah. For the next half hour, we wandered through the streets of Verona, listening to Romeo go on and on about this Rosaline character. And the play wasn't even named after her.

"He's got it bad," said Frankie.

"More than bad," I chuckled. "His brain's fried. But, if Romeo is all goopy about Rosaline, maybe we should try to find Juliet. You know, to get them together? Otherwise, this play will never end, and we'll never get home!"

Frankie nodded. "Good idea. Um, hey, Benvolio?"

But Benvolio was suddenly crouching in a doorway. "Look yonder, my friends," he said. "Here comes Capulet and some young man with a sword—"

We looked down the street.

"Again with the swords!" said Frankie. "Don't you people have regular sports?"

Benvolio paused to give her a strange look, then said, "We cannot risk another street battle. Perhaps we shall see one another soon. For now, I must take my lovesick cousin away from here. Montagues and Capulets are like oil and water. There's no mixing them! Be careful!"

With that, Benvolio trotted away, tugging the sighing Romeo with him. Before we could make tracks ourselves, Mr. Capulet saw us.

"You there! You with the book!" he shouted, motioning to Frankie. "Come here at once!"

Since the guy with him had a sword, Frankie and I decided to do what he said.

# Chapter 4

"I need you for a task," Mr. Capulet said to us. "Stand by my house there, and do not leave!"

He pointed to a big stone house with lots of windows, a walled garden, and a balcony overlooking the garden.

Obeying, we stood in front of it.

"This looks like the balcony on the stage at school," I said. "I wonder if we get to climb up."

"Not if they can help it," whispered Frankie, pointing to lots of guardy types standing around with long speary things. "People sure like to make with the sharp and pointy in Verona, don't they, Dev?"

"Which tells me we shouldn't mess with them. So this is old man Capulet's house?"

Frankie glanced at the book and nodded. "If I'm reading this right, the fight in the square and meeting Romeo was in act one, scene one, right at the very beginning of the play. Now we're in act one, scene two. And, yeah, it's supposed to be at Capulet's house."

"Acts and scenes instead of chapters?" I said. "Plays are sort of strange, aren't they?"

She nodded. "What's even stranger is that plays are almost totally people talking. You only know what the people are thinking by what they say."

I thought about that. "If a play is mostly people talking, then we should probably listen to what Capulet and the other guy are saying, right?"

Frankie grinned. "A plan. I like it. Let's listen."

I tugged up my tights as we leaned over and listened.

And boy did we get an earful!

"My lord Capulet," the young man was saying, "I love your daughter, Juliet. I wish to marry her."

"Holy crow, Frankie!" I whispered. "Juliet is Capulet's daughter!"

"And Romeo is a Montague," she said. "I begin to see the problem in this story. Let's listen some more."

Old Capulet stroked his beard. "My child is yet a stranger in the world, dear Paris. She does not know you well enough yet. But I have an idea. This night I hold an old accustomed feast. I have invited many a guest."

I nudged Frankie. "Do you hear that? A party! I do great at parties! All the food, the fun, the people, the food. Plus, of course, all the food, which is my personal specialty, if I may sayeth so—"

"Devin," growled Frankie. "There is a play going on here. . . ."

"It shall be a costume party," said Capulet. "So, Paris, I ask you to come tonight. Woo my Juliet, win her heart. If you can win her, then I grant that you may marry her. What do you say to that?"

Almost like a ballet dancer, Paris did a small twinkly leap in the air. "Thank you, my lord. I shall be there!"

The next moment, he was running off chirping about what sort of costume he would wear.

I turned to Frankie. "Talk about mix-ups. We have Romeo all gooey about Rosaline, and Paris all twinkly about Juliet. I think we have our work cut out for us—"

"Now, then, you two!" said Capulet. "Come here!"

I cringed. "I hope he's not going to slice and dice—"

But instead of tugging out a sword, he tugged a sheet of folded paper from the pocket of his robe. "I called you over because I see you have a book. I presume you must be able to read."

"Read?" said Frankie, waving the book around. "Sometimes our English teacher Mr. Wexler's not so sure."

"But we try," I said. "When we can understand the words."

The old guy squinted at us. "Yes, well, good. I have a little errand I'd like you to do. Go about fair Verona, and find the people whose names are written on this sheet. Tell them there is a great feast at my house tonight. And that they should come in costume! Now, run along!"

He hustled back into his house, barking out orders for his servants to begin preparations.

"You know what's weird, Devin?" Frankie asked.

"Actually, the shorter list is what's *not* weird," I said.

"I agree. But what's really weird is that, by themselves the Capulets and the Montagues seem like fairly nice folks. The problem is, when they get together they can't stop fighting."

I nodded. "Wouldn't it be cool if we could stop it? Like if we get Romeo and Juliet together, maybe the Montys and the Caps will stop fighting."

Frankie's eyes grew wide. "What a great idea!"

"I thought it up myself," I said, as we headed to the town square. "Plus, I like happy endings."

"My personal fave, too," Frankie said with a grin.

"Okay, then, first of all, if we're playing parts in a play, let's play our part by trying to find the people on Capulet's list."

"Frankie, that was beautiful. Read that list!"

But when Frankie unfolded Mr. Capulet's paper and scanned the writing, she stopped, blinked, held it up to her nose, blinked again, turned the paper upside down, blinked a third time, rubbed her eyes, blinked yet again, then gave out a long, low grumble.

"What's the prob?" I asked.

"I can't read this!"

"Why not?"

"Because, it's . . . in Italian!"

I grabbed the sheet from her and peered at the words. "Whoa. Headache City! I guess we need to find someone who knows the words. But who do we know that doesn't want to wave a long pointy sword our way—"

Frankie grinned suddenly. "I know who! Romeo!"

I turned and there he was, the hero of the story, doing his famous zigzag walk along a side street on the far side of the square. Benvolio was straggling behind him, rolling his eyes and muttering to himself.

"Hey, guys!" called Frankie. "Can you read?"

For the first time since we met him, Romeo cracked a smile. Pointing to the book in my hand, he said, "Ay, if I know the letters and the language. Cannot you read?"

"Of course we can," I said. "But pretty much only English, and sometimes not even that. Anyway, Mr. Capulet gave us this list and it's in the wrong language."

"Capulet?" said Benvolio. "Ho-ho, a secret letter from the Capulets. This will be good. Read it, Romeo."

Romeo took the paper from Frankie, snapped it open, and began to scan it. "Ah, yes. Names are written here. Signore Martino and his wife and daughters, the young gentleman Paris—"

"We just saw him," said Frankie.

"—the widow Vitruvio, Signore Placentio, Mercutio and his brother Valentine, Tybalt—"

"Tybalt?" snorted Benvolio. "What sort of list is this?"

"The guest list to a party at the Capulets' tonight," said Frankie. "You guys should definitely go. And Romeo might even see someone he likes."

"It's far too dangerous to go into the house of our enemy," said Benvolio. "The Capulets will want to fight instead of dance. And we shall be recognized."

"Not if you wear a mask," said Frankie. "And did I mention that Capulet's daughter Juliet will be there?"

"Never heard of her," said Romeo.

"Something tells me you will," I said with a little chuckle. "The word is that she's a babe. Everybody wants to marry her. But you can't let that happen."

"Why not?" asked Romeo, still scanning the paper.

"Trust us," said Frankie. "You gotta see her, you were meant for her. She's . . . she's . . . well, I don't know what she is yet, but you just gotta!"

Romeo shrugged and read out more of the list. "Someone named Livia is invited. And Lucio, Helena, Rosaline—" He stopped. "The fair and beautiful Rosaline will be there? *My* Rosaline?"

I was going to tell him that he should definitely forget about her, but an idea was beginning to form in my noggin. I remember, because I don't get that many ideas, and it always sort of hurts when I do.

"You bet Rosaline will be there!" I told him.

Romeo tilted his head. "Rosaline at this party. . . ."

Benvolio grinned. "Romeo, are you thinking—"

"No, no," said Romeo.

"Too bad. It would be fun—"

"I'm done thinking!" said Romeo. "We shall go. You and Frankie and Devin and me. And you shall all see just how wonderful and sweet my fair Rosaline is!"

Frankie winked at me. "Or, just maybe you'll meet someone even more beautiful than Rosaline. . . ."

Romeo laughed. "That can never be! The

all-seeing sun ne'er saw her match since the world begun—"

"Enough!" said Benvolio, sticking his fingers in his ears.

Still laughing, Romeo turned. "I'll go to this party and rejoice in the splendor of my Rosaline!"

With that, he raced away into a side street, up an alley, and was gone, his pal Benvolio reluctantly chasing at his heels.

Frankie smiled. "Are we matchmakers or are we matchmakers?"

"We are matchmakers!" I said, slapping her five.

"I'm feeling pretty good right about now."

But someone else wasn't feeling so good.

"Nurse!" someone cried out. "Nurse! Help! Nurse!"

The shouting came from the Capulet house.

Frankie gasped. "What if it's Juliet? What if she's sick?"

"She can't be sick," I said, "or all our matchmaking plans have been for nothing. We'd better flip ahead—"

"Whoa, Devin—"

There was a reason Frankie didn't want me to flip ahead. Flipping was dangerous. It could cause a sudden story meltdown. It was like skipping pages in a book.

And that's against the rules.

But sometimes you gotta bend the rules a little.

"Nurse!" came another cry.

"I'm doing it!" I said.

"Okay, but just one page!" said Frankie. "Do it!"

I did it.

Flip.

*Kkkkk!*

Lightning flashed across the sky.

# Chapter 5

*Kkkk!* Everything went dark, then light, then Frankie and I went crashing into the next scene.

We tumbled out onto a tile floor, twisting up my tights and upsetting the pillow arrangement of Frankie's weirdo headgear.

We looked up. It was obviously a girl's bedroom, all pink and frilly, with a balcony overlooking the garden.

But it wasn't Juliet doing the yelling. It was Mrs. Capulet, storming back and forth, booming at the top of her lungs, "Nurse!"

"What's the problem, Mrs. C?" said Frankie. "You don't look like you need a nurse, but maybe you'd better lie down—"

The woman gave us the old "you sillyhead" look. "Take your hands off me. Nothing is wrong with me. I was calling for the nurse."

Frankie frowned at her. Then her eyes lit up. "Wait a sec. By nurse, do you mean like a nanny?"

"Exactly," said Mrs. Capulet. And she started up again. "Nurse! Nurse, please come in here—"

"Yes, ma'am!" called a voice, and in hustled a middle-aged woman, all disheveled and rumpled. Her face was plump and red as she swept breathlessly into the room.

She bowed to Mrs. Capulet, wiped her hands on her apron, and said, "Yes, my lady? What is it?"

"Find my daughter," Mrs. Capulet said.

"Your daughter. Of course, my lady," said the nurse. "Oh, but I remember when the child was just a toddler—toddling around the room, she was. Since that time it has been years—oh, I remember a year once—"

"Spare me!" said Mrs. Capulet. "Just find her!"

"Yes, ma'am." The nurse bowed, hustled out of the room, made some noise, called out a few times, and finally came back. Running into the room behind her was a teenage girl.

Frankie gasped softly. "It's her. It's Juliet."

The girl was young, but tall, with long brown hair tightly braided and tied up in double loops in the back. She wore a gown of light pink that trailed behind her as she walked.

"Yes, mother," she said, bowing. "What is your will?"

Even I had to admit that Juliet was definitely cute. She smiled at me and Frankie, then waited quietly for her mother to speak.

"The reason I've asked you here," said her mother, "is because . . . oh, dear, now, let me see—"

"I remember when our Juliet was a little thing!" the nurse interrupted. "She was four or five and she had a blanket that she pulled around with her everywhere and I said—"

"Enough!" cried Mrs. Capulet, rolling her eyes. "Hold your peace, nurse, if you please! Now, Juliet, the reason for which I called you—"

The nurse went on. "Yet I cannot choose but laugh about young Juliet and that blanket dragging around until it was nearly black with grime—for the mud brought in from the streets—there was a wedding that day—"

"Wedding!" said Juliet's mother. "That's it! That's just what I want to talk about today, Juliet. Tell me, daughter Juliet, how stands your disposition to be married?"

Juliet, who had been waiting patiently, now stood

up straight, her eyes growing large. A moment later, she sat down on the corner of her bed and looked up at her mother. "Married? It is an honor that I dream not of."

"Think of marriage now," said her mother. "For the valiant gentleman, Paris, seeks you for his love. What say you?"

Juliet seemed a little overloaded. I glanced over at Frankie and she was sort of in shock, too.

Married? I mean, *eeeww!* And Paris was, like, totally the wrong guy.

Juliet blinked up at her mom, but couldn't seem to say anything.

"Well, this night you shall behold him at our feast," Mrs. Capulet went on, edging for the door. "Read young Paris's face. This precious book of love only lacks a cover—"

There was the sudden clanking and clattering of pots and pans from downstairs.

"The party begins," said Mrs. Capulet. "Juliet, our guests will begin to arrive soon. Make haste!"

With that, Mrs. Capulet swept out of the room, the nurse running after her.

Frankie kicked me, I guess that was my cue. "Um, hi, Jules," I said, "I'm Devin."

"And I'm his pal, Frankie," said Frankie. "We were . . . sent to help you pick an outfit."

Did I mention that Frankie was good at thinking fast?

"It is so nice to meet you." Juliet smiled at us, then ran to her closet and pulled out a bunch of gowns, throwing them on the bed. "Now . . . which one should I choose?"

Frankie went over. "I like the greenish one. It makes you look mysterious."

"I do like it," said Juliet softly.

"And I like parties," I said. "Who said Shakespeare wasn't fun?"

"I'm pretty sure that was you, Devin," said Frankie. "Of course, that was before you started wearing tights—"

There was a sudden stomping noise outside the room. Someone heavy was tramping up the stairs and muttering something about a mess-up with the guest list.

Frankie and I shot looks at each other.

"Uh-oh," said Frankie, "that sounds like your dad. He thinks we're out rounding up the party guests, which we sort of didn't do."

"My father is sometimes quick to anger," said Juliet.

"So can we hide here?" I asked.

Juliet grinned. "I have a better idea." She dragged a box out of the back of the closet and threw open the lid. Inside were dozens of masks of all different kinds. There were birds and tigers, giraffes and gnomes.

"Choose one for each of you, and escape over the balcony into the garden. You can enter the party from there. I use the balcony all the time when I want to sneak out. And the best part is that my father will not recognize you!"

"Hey, thanks, Jules," I said. "You are pretty cool."

"Now, shoo! Shoo! I must get ready."

We yanked a couple of masks out of the chest, clambered over the marble balcony, and climbed down the tree that coiled up from the flower garden below.

Mr. Capulet came storming into Juliet's room.

"Hurry!" said Frankie.

"Hey, climbing is not so easy when you're all twisted up in skintight tights, you know!" I jumped the last few feet to the ground below.

"As if it's a picnic wearing a dress longer than a bedsheet," said Frankie. "This balcony could definitely use a ladder."

"Or an elevator!" I grunted.

The sun was going down quickly, casting shadows in the curving streets outside the Capulet house. The party was just getting into full swing. Music was playing. There was the clank and ping of dishes, which meant lots of munchies for me.

We pulled our masks over our faces. Mine was in the shape of a monkey. Frankie wore a bird's face.

"Get ready for the big scene," I said. "Where Romeo and Juliet finally meet!"

"It's going to be cool," said Frankie. "But keep a lookout for Romeo. I hope he doesn't chicken out and fly away."

"This, coming from a person wearing a beak," I said.

Then, just as we were about to enter the house, we heard a bunch of young men stumbling along the street behind us. They were all dressed in masks, except one. But we probably would have recognized him just from the noises he was making.

He was sighing like a leaky balloon.

"Oh, dear me! Oh, me, me, me!"

I laughed. "Here comes Romeo. In a few minutes he'll meet Juliet and then—fireworks!"

"Maybe those fireworks are going to fizzle out," said Frankie. "It looks like I was right. Romeo's trying to get away!"

# Chapter 6

By the time we reached Romeo, he had already started to walk away. His buddies tried to convince him to go to the party, but he was one tough sell.

"I will not go," said Romeo with a sigh.

One of his pals removed his mask. He was short and lively, with a big, smiling face. He looked like he just wanted to have a good time.

"But, Romeo!" he said. "We must have you dance!"

"Mercutio," said Romeo, shaking his head wearily at this new character. "You have dancing shoes with nimble soles. I have a soul of lead. It weighs me to the ground. I cannot move."

Mercutio laughed. "But you are in love. Lovers have Cupid's wings to help them soar above the ground!"

"Good one!" I said.

I had to admit, I sort of liked this new character.

The Capulet shindig was getting louder by the minute. We heard even more clinking of silverware and glasses.

"Soon, the dancing will be done," said Benvolio, peeking into a side window. "Supper is already started! We shall come too late."

Romeo peered over Benvolio's shoulder into the Capulets' living room. "My mind tells me the stars are not right for a visit to our enemy's house . . . but if everyone else is going . . . then I suppose I will go, too."

"That's the spirit!" cried Mercutio, grabbing Romeo, Frankie, and me by the arm and pushing us to the front door. "Put on your masks, gentlemen, and young lady, and in we go!"

We all put on our masks—Romeo's was a tiger— and marched to the front of the Capulets' house, slipped past all the heavily armed guards as if we were Capulets ourselves, and strode into the front room.

I tell you, this room was something. It was like an exhibit in an old-house museum, but all aglow with life. Candles blazed everywhere, shedding their light on about a hundred people. In the corner, a small combo was playing strange-shaped instruments. But everyone seemed to think it was good dance music. They twirled across the floor.

"Devin," Frankie said to me. "I know it's weird, but I feel like dancing."

My feet started tapping, too. But I resisted. "If you see somebody tripping on his face, that would be me. Besides, monkeys don't dance."

Soon, the band finished its number, and Mr. Capulet started tapping a glass to get everyone's attention.

"Welcome, everyone. Welcome!"

I nudged Frankie. "He wouldn't say that if he knew some Montagues were here."

"Welcome to my house!" he went on. "There is plenty of food and much dancing to be had this evening. So, bring in more light and move the tables away. Quench the hearth fires. For we shall dance. Play, musicians, play!"

The music resumed with a fast tune, and everybody began twirling.

Suddenly, Romeo cornered Frankie and me. He pointed across the room, then took a deep breath as if he were going to come out with something big. He sure did.

"You see that young woman dancing there?" he said. "It seems she hangs upon the cheek of night as a rich jewel. For I never saw true beauty till this night!"

I squinted through the moving crowd. "Please don't tell me it's Rosaline?"

"Who is this Rosaline you speak of?" Romeo asked.

Frankie laughed. "Your crush? The one you were all gaga over this morning?"

Romeo laughed. "There was no morning until now."

He slipped away through the spinning crowd, and we spotted who he had been looking at.

It was Juliet. She was dancing in her green gown.

She looked amazing.

"This is it, Devin," Frankie whispered. "This is where they meet."

"This is so cool. It's like a historic moment. It's like . . . hey, it's like that historic moment when you and I met."

Frankie grumbled. "Devin, we met at a hot-dog picnic. We were three. You got mustard all over me."

I gazed off into the distance. "And you never got that stain out, did you? I told you it was historic."

"Thanks for the memories. Now pay attention."

But I couldn't. There was a rustling behind me and suddenly someone pushed me out of the way.

"That man there—" snarled a voice.

We turned to see that tall man in the black tunic again. He hadn't even bothered to change for the party. Except that now he was wearing the mask of a panther.

I nudged Frankie. "It's that Tybalt guy. The angry one from the first scene."

"I remember," she whispered.

Tybalt had old Capulet by the arm. "I tell you, he sounds like a . . . a . . . Montague! Someone get me my sword! It is Romeo!"

Mr. Capulet growled. "Tybalt, why do you rave so?"

"Look there, uncle!" Tybalt growled, pointing at Romeo with one hand and gripping his sword with the other. "That is a Montague, our foe. He is a villain come to scorn at us this night—"

Capulet grunted. "Young Romeo, is it?"

"'Tis he, that villain Romeo," hissed Tybalt. "I shall—"

"You shall do nothing," said Capulet firmly. "Let him alone. To say truth, all Verona brags of him to be a virtuous and well-governed youth. This is my house. Take no note of him—"

"I'll not endure him!"

"He shall be endured!" Capulet replied. "What? Am I the master of this house, or you?"

Tybalt looked as if his head was going to pop.

"Go peacefully, Tybalt," said Capulet, "and do not mind Romeo. This is my house! More light there!

More light!" He strode off to see the servingmen. But Tybalt stood there, staring at Romeo and hissing like a snake.

"Oh, this makes me rage!" said Tybalt. He backed off into the shadows, folded his arms, and began to sulk without ever once taking his eyes off Romeo, even though the crowd of dancers came between them.

"Devin, I don't like that guy," said Frankie. "The way he's looking at Romeo and clutching that sword of his. He's like some kind of wild animal."

"No kidding. He's got the mask to prove it."

Meanwhile, Romeo was dancing his way across the room to Juliet. Frankie and I pretended to do the same. Pretty soon, we were near them.

"Listen up, Devin," said Frankie. "They're talking."

Romeo took Juliet's hand and began to dance with her. Looking directly into her eyes like they do on mushy TV shows, he took her hand and said, "If I profane with my unworthiest hand this holy shrine, the gentle sin is this: my lips, two blushing pilgrims, ready stand to smooth that rough touch with a tender kiss."

Frankie sighed. "That's beautiful—"

"Like a greeting card," I said. "And the best part is, I almost understood it: He's saying that if his hand is too rough, he'll kiss her hand and smooth it out.

Extremely icky, of course, but the guy knows his pretty words."

"I think it means he likes her."

"She likes him too," I said. "Check it out."

Juliet was giving Romeo a little smile. "Good pilgrim, you do wrong your hand too much . . . for saints have hands that pilgrims' hands do touch, and palm to palm is holy palmers' kiss."

It was love at first sight.

Too bad nasty Tybalt had Romeo in his sights.

Throughout this whole scene, the guy kept stewing up a storm there in the shadows. And I was worried.

I mean, here we were in total enemy territory.

And here was a Montague, giving a Capulet a kiss! It was like a call to war!

Suddenly, the nurse hustled over to the dancing couple. "Madam, your mother wants a word with you."

"So soon?" said Romeo.

"I must obey," said Juliet. She sighed and scampered off to her mother's table.

Romeo came over to us. "Who is her mother?"

That's when it hit us. Romeo didn't have a clue.

"Whoa, hold on to your mask, Romeo," I said. "Juliet's mother is—are you ready—Mrs. Capulet—"

Romeo gasped. "Is she a Capulet? Then . . . my love . . . is my enemy?"

"Sorry, guy," said Frankie. "But that's the way it is."

"And speaking of enemies," I said, keeping my eye on Tybalt, who was circling around us now, "I think it would be a really primo idea to get ourselves out of here."

I guess Benvolio had the same idea, because he came edging through the crowd at that moment, too, grabbed Romeo's arm and pulled him to the door. "Come now. We've eaten our fill. All that's left is Tybalt."

While Benvolio and Mercutio pulled him quickly from the house, Romeo kept searching out the crowd for another glimpse of Juliet.

Just after he slipped away, she sprung out of the shadows, touching Frankie on the arm. "Tell me!" she said. "Who is that young man you are following?"

Frankie told her. "His name is Romeo. And I hate to be the one to break it to you, but . . . Romeo is a Montague—"

She uttered a short gasp. "Oh, no! My only love sprung from my only hate! That I must love a loathed enemy!" With that, she went flitting off into the depths of the house.

Frankie turned to me. "This isn't going to be easy."

"But the play is just beginning," I said. "Maybe it

gets easier later on. These two are meant to be together. Otherwise, Shakespeare wouldn't have named his play after them."

Frankie glanced at how much of the play there was still to come. "I hope you're right."

A moment later, old Capulet gave the order and all the torches were put out.

And so were we.

Into the street. Where we saw Benvolio and Mercutio, but not Romeo.

"Where is he?" asked Frankie.

"I think he hath hid himself among some trees," said Benvolio. "Let us go. 'Tis vain to seek him here that means not to be found. Good night, Devin . . . Frankie . . ."

Together Mercutio and Benvolio wandered off into the night.

"Now what?" said Frankie.

We didn't have to wait long for an answer. At that moment, we heard that old familiar sigh.

"Oh . . . oh," said Romeo.

"Uh-oh," said Frankie.

Because the sighs were coming from right inside the Capulet garden.

# Chapter 7

Frankie and I stood in the street, staring at the stone wall surrounding the Capulet garden. It was about ten feet high, with sharp spikes running along the top.

"How did Romeo get in there?" I asked.

Frankie laughed. "If that look in his eyes when he saw Juliet meant anything, he probably jumped over the wall in a single bound!"

"The guy should be playing pro basketball," I said. Then I eyed those pointy spikes again. "Wait a sec. Don't tell me we have to jump that wall. Because, I tell you, in these tights, that would not be pretty."

By the light of the moon, Frankie read a page of the book, then gave me a sick sort of grin. "Sorry, Dev."

"Besides which," I went on, "good old Tybalt

could find us in there. He can't wait to do some serious damage with that sword of his. And in case you wondered, my sword is still fairly plastic."

"We have to climb over," she said. "We have to make sure Romeo and Tybalt don't meet up. Plus, this is a big scene, and we have to be there."

"I just hope it's not my death scene!" I said.

Frankie grinned, then put her hands together and gave me a boost—okay, sometimes she's stronger—and I scrambled up the wall and over the side.

*Thwump!* I crumpled to the ground next to Romeo.

*Thwump!* Frankie clambered over a second later.

The garden we were in was small and square and filled with tall gangly plants and big fluffy flowers. Above us hung Juliet's balcony. Just for the record, it was about twenty feet high, with all kinds of branches and vines creeping up to it from the garden below.

Even in the dim light coming from inside, I could see Romeo gazing up at Juliet's room.

"Oh, I see where this is going," I said, giving him a nudge. "You want to see her again. And hey, I'm all for that. But you should probably arrange to see her somewhere a bit safer. It's totally dangerous here."

With his eyeballs still fixed on Juliet's balcony, Romeo whispered, "How can I leave, when my heart is here?"

"Romeo," said Frankie, "as weird as it sounds, Devin is right. Juliet is a Capulet. And you know who else is a Capulet? Tybalt."

"You remember him," I said. "Angry guy? Shouts a lot? Wears black all the time? Well, Tybalt's gunning for us. I mean, he's swording for us. And I, for one, don't want to be the first-ever Italian shish kebab!"

Of course, Romeo didn't budge. He just kept staring up at that balcony. Suddenly, there was a flicker of candlelight, and Juliet's room grew brighter.

"But soft!" said Romeo. "What light through yonder window breaks? It is the east, and Juliet is the sun."

The latch on the balcony window clicked, and Juliet, looking all airy and light, stepped out onto the balcony.

"It is my lady," whispered Romeo. "It is my love! O, that she knew she were!"

Even in the light from the moon and stars, Juliet's cheeks seemed to glow pink from the dancing.

"The brightness of her cheek would shame the stars as daylight doth a lamp," the lovesick guy went on. "Her eyes in heaven would through the airy region stream so bright that birds would sing and think it were not night—"

Step by step, Romeo drew closer, as if he was drawn toward her and couldn't help it.

"She must be magnetic," I said.

"Plus, he's in love," said Frankie.

Now, normally, both Frankie and I would be reaching for the gagging spoon right about now, or beginning self-choking procedures, but I guess we really didn't feel that way now. Already I wanted Romeo and Juliet to get together. I mean, neither of them really fit in with the folks around them, and the odds were so stacked against them, you sort of wanted them to win out.

Juliet leaned against the balcony railing and looked out over Verona, not saying anything. She didn't have to. Romeo filled in all the downtime with more poetry!

"See how she leans her cheek upon her hand!" he whispered with emotion. "O, that I were a glove upon that hand, that I might touch that cheek."

"Now he wants to be a glove," I whispered.

"Isn't it romantic?" murmured Frankie, taking out the book.

"Better than being a shoe, I guess. . . ."

Juliet sighed. "Ah, me!"

"Shh! She speaks!" gasped Romeo. "O, speak again, bright angel!'

Juliet was quiet for a moment, then said, "O, Romeo, Romeo! wherefore art thou Romeo?"

"He's right here!" I whispered.

"Devin," whispered Frankie. "*Wherefore* means

'why.' She's asking why he has to be a Montague—"

"Deny thy father and refuse thy name," Juliet said. "Or if thou wilt not, be but sworn my love, and I'll no longer be a Capulet."

"Shall I hear more, or shall I speak?" asked Romeo.

"Well, if you ask me," I said. "I would—"

Frankie tapped the page. "Believe me, Devin, he's not asking you!"

"What's Montague?" said Juliet. "It is not hand nor foot nor arm nor face. O, be some other name. What's in a name? That which we call a rose by any other name would smell as sweet. O, Romeo, refuse thy name—"

"Henceforth I never will be Romeo!" Romeo blurted out, stepping out of the shadows and standing right under Juliet's balcony.

The girl practically choked. "What man art thou?"

"I know not how to tell thee who I am," he replied. "My name, dear saint, is hateful to myself, because it is an enemy to thee."

Juliet leaned over the balcony and blinked down into the garden. "My ears have not yet drunk a hundred words, and yet I know the sound!" Her eyes glistened in the moonlight. "Art thou not Romeo, and a Montague?"

"Neither," he said, "if either thee dislike."

"How camest thou hither, tell me? The orchard walls are high and hard to climb, and the place death, considering who thou art, if any of my kinsmen find thee here."

"With love's light wings did I over-perch these walls," said Romeo. "For stony limits cannot hold love out, and what love can do, *that* dares love attempt. Therefore thy kinsmen are no stop to me. . . ."

"We tried to tell him of the danger," said Frankie. "But the guy has only one thing on his mind."

"And just so there isn't any confusion," I said, "the thing he has on his mind is . . . you!"

Juliet laughed. "Romeo, you brought your friends with you. . . ."

"He couldn't stop us," I said.

"And we couldn't stop him," said Frankie.

Juliet blushed in the moonlight. "O, gentle Romeo, if thou dost love, pronounce it faithfully."

"What shall I swear by?"

"Juliet!" called a voice from inside.

"I hear some noise within!" said Juliet. "Dear love, adieu! I will come again."

"Stay for a minute!" said Romeo.

"I can't, " she said. "If you do want to marry me, send word tomorrow. I'll send a messenger to find you. Tell them the time and place . . . and I will marry you!"

"Whoa, that was quick!" I said.

"Things move fast in Shakespeare," said Frankie.

"Juliet!" It was the nurse's voice, getting closer.

"Coming!" she called back. "Romeo, I will send someone for your word."

He grinned from ear to ear. "I'll be waiting!"

"Good night, good night! Parting is such sweet sorrow that I shall say good night till it be tomorrow!"

"I don't think we have that much time," I said. "I think I hear someone outside the garden. What if it's Tybalt—"

Juliet made a soft sort of giggle at Romeo, then dashed in and closed the window behind her.

Romeo fell back into the shadows, a big smile on his face. "Juliet will marry me," he said. "And it must be done quickly before her family can stop us. I must seek help in our little scheme. And I know just the person. I know a friar friend of mine."

"A fryer? You know a chicken?"

Romeo laughed. "Not a chicken. A friar is a monk. Let's go."

We did go. And because things were happening fast, by the next page, we were there.

# Chapter 8

It was nearly morning, and we were on a dirt road heading out of the city. The countryside around us was beautiful. On each side were big meadows and rolling hills, and here and there little stone houses with gardens and bunches of sheep and goats grazing.

"Frankie," I said, taking it all in, "after last night, this is like one of those summer mornings when you wake up and realize the world is a nifty place."

She grinned. "I like the postcardiness of it all."

"Check it out," I said. "I mean, here we are in old Verona. We have no homework hanging over our heads. The birds are tweeting. The air is clean. The sheepies go *baaa*. 'And the grey-eyed morn smiles on

59

the frowning night, checking the eastern clouds with streaks of light!'"

She paused and turned to me. "Devin, that's like poetry."

"Like?" I said. "Ha! It *is* poetry! When you weren't looking, I was doing some serious reading—"

"You weren't!"

"I was!" I held up the book, which I'd snuck out of Frankie's pocket as Romeo led us out of the city. "And even though it was tough going, I picked up some of the words. It's starting to rub off on me. Frankie, I'm learning to speak Shakespeare!"

"Mr. Wexler will be so pleased," she said.

Romeo stopped in front of a tiny stone hut by the roadside. Next to the hut was a long garden thick with flowers and low leafy plants. Romeo froze.

"What is it?" I asked.

"The friar is coming!" he said, suddenly scampering behind a tree next to the hut. He put his finger to his lips. "Let's surprise him with the happy news!"

Frankie nudged me. "Romeo is, like, super-happy that he met Juliet."

"And we helped," I said, handing her the book again. "I guess you'd call the balcony scene their first date?"

"And here they are, already wanting to get married!"

I sighed. "Kids today. Don't get me started."

The moment we crowded behind the tree with Romeo, we began to hear humming. It was a man's low, growly sort of humming, very off-key.

And there he was, coming around from the back of the hut—a short, plump guy, wearing a hooded brown robe, and carrying a basket the size of a bathtub.

"That's Friar Laurence!" whispered Romeo. "He is talking to himself. He always does this. Let us listen. . . ."

"Before the sun dries up the dew, I must collect these flowers and weeds," the chubby friar was saying. "Oh, yes, in plants and herbs there is precious juice. Healing and healthful juice for the body and the mind. . . ."

Friar Laurence stooped over and picked a small flower. "Within this tender blossom, for instance, is both poison and medicine. Smell it, it cheers you up. Taste it, and you fall into a deep sleep that looks like death itself!"

"He talks to himself a lot," I said.

"Our book calls it a soliloquy," Frankie whispered.

I chuckled. "Sosillyquy? Because it's so silly to talk to yourself?"

She turned to me. "I don't think so, Devin—whoa!"

Grabbing our hands, Romeo jumped out of hiding

and leaped in front of the friar. "Good morrow, Father!"

The friar turned. "Oh! Romeo! You startled me. Oh, my poor heart! Well, well, up early, I see. And with friends?"

"I'm Devin. This is Frankie," I said, bowing.

"Welcome to you all," the friar replied. "I see, our Romeo hath not been in bed tonight."

Our friend smiled. "I was feasting with my enemy."

"Capulet's party?" said the monk. "You were there?"

"Not only was I there," Romeo said with a quick nod, "I was wounded and need your medicines."

The friar gasped. "Wounded?"

"Wounded in the heart," said Romeo, with his smile turning into a kind of distant gaze. "By Juliet, daughter of my sworn enemy."

"Talk about a crush," said Frankie. "This guy was flattened by a Capulet. And for the record, Juliet is pretty nuts about him, too."

"And the reason I'm here," said Romeo, peeking into the friar's little hut, "is to ask you to marry us. . . ."

The friar dropped his basket. *Thunk!*

"Today," said Romeo, grinning.

From the look on the friar's face, I bet if he had still been holding that basket, he would have dropped it again.

"Today?" he coughed. "Today!"

Friar Laurence was obviously having a real problem getting his head around this. "But what about sweet Rosaline?"

"Hey, we said the same thing," I told the guy. "Romeo doesn't even remember her. And you gotta admit, Rosaline doesn't even seem to show up in the play. I mean, here we are in act two, scene two and—"

"Play?" said the friar, his eyes wide. "Act? Scene?"

Then I remembered that people in the books we get dropped into don't really know anything about their being in a book. It's their life, that's all. I decided not to rock the boat. "I mean, you know, this play . . . of life!"

"Ah!" said the friar. "I know exactly what you mean. Well, so, come with me, Romeo. There may be something in this. You are young, but not too young, I suppose. And a marriage might solve the terrible hatred between your Montagues and her Capulets. Yes, yes. Let's talk. . . ."

He drew Romeo off into his hut.

"Ah, yes," said Frankie with a smile. "Old Friar Laurence, the wedding planner—"

There was, behind us, a sudden rustle of leaves and crackle of branches.

"Uh-oh," I said. "Someone's coming."

Frankie whirled around. "Not bad guys with

swords and looks on their faces that say 'get Devin and Frankie'?"

Actually, it turned out to be Juliet's nurse.

"Romeo!" she shouted, huffing and puffing. "Boy!"

Leaving the friar inside, Romeo came out of the hut.

"A word with you, Romeo," said the nurse, catching her breath. "My young lady bade me find you."

"I have been waiting for her message," said Romeo. "What does she say?"

"I'll tell you in a moment," the nurse replied. "But first, let me say this." She put on a harsh expression. "If you hurt my Juliet, it would be a terrible thing. She is young and gentle and I care for her and I will not forget a terrible hurt to her."

"I care for her, too," said Romeo. "With all my heart."

The nurse breathed in deeply, then nodded. "Good. I will tell her that."

"And tell her this," said Romeo. "To come this afternoon to Friar Laurence's cell . . . to be married."

"Married?" she gasped. "Oh, truly?"

"Truly," said Frankie with a grin. "He's serious."

I nodded. "In fact, he even hired Friar Laurence to plan the wedding. It'll be this afternoon."

Well, the nurse smiled so big that her grin just

about met behind her ears. "Juliet shall be there!" she said.

"And after dark tonight," said Romeo, "I will arrange to visit her at her house. Her family will not see me."

"And Frankie and I will be lookouts," I said. "Tybalt is, like, everywhere. Plus, if Mr. Capulet sees you, he won't exactly throw a party for you, either."

"Throw a sword, maybe," said Frankie.

"And another thing," I said. "Unless you plan to spend the rest of the day practicing the high jump, maybe you should think about bringing some kind of ladder to get over the wall and up the balcony."

"Good point," said Frankie. "And if we keep following you around, I want an easier way up that wall."

Romeo's eyes lit up. "Splendid idea, my friends. Find a rope ladder and set it up in Juliet's garden for tonight."

"Just the thing!" said the nurse. "I shall tell Juliet what we have said here. But sir, you must know that the nobleman, Paris, has asked for Juliet's hand in marriage. He will not like this. Neither will Juliet's cousin Tybalt."

Romeo smiled, but his thoughts were somewhere else. "Thank you for the warning. Now, give my love to thy lady. We meet later."

"A thousand times, sir!" she said, and hustled back down the dusty road toward the city gates.

As Romeo headed back into the Friar's hut, Frankie turned to me. "Dev, it looks like the scene is ending. What do you want to do?"

"How about we go find a ladder?" I said. "I mean, it's strange, but Romeo and Juliet seem to like us and trust us. We actually seem to have a real part in this play."

"Just like Mr. Wexler wanted," said Frankie. "Let's go find a ladder!"

So, as best we could in our funny clothes, we raced each other back to the city.

# Chapter 9

It was amazingly easy to find a rope ladder.

There was one just sitting in a pile of trash behind a row of shops. It was as if we were meant to find it.

The ladder was not in great shape, but we figured it would hold our weight the next time we hauled ourselves over that garden wall.

After that, Frankie and I got totally lost.

The streets of Verona snaked around here and there and crisscrossed like a spiderweb. Trying to find our way back to the Capulet house, Frankie and I felt like mice in a maze.

Luckily, we met our old friends Benvolio and Mercutio on the way.

"Hey, dudes!" I said. "Are we glad to see you!"

"Ah, Frankie and Devin," said Mercutio. "Have you seen our elusive friend Romeo?"

I glanced at Frankie. I wasn't sure whether these guys were supposed to know about Romeo and Juliet yet.

"Um . . . maybe," I said.

"He left us high and dry last night," said Benvolio. "And so he probably doesn't know that Tybalt—"

"Tybalt," Mercutio interrupted, "that angry prince of cats—"

"What about Tybalt?" asked Frankie.

"He has sent a challenge to Montague," said Benvolio. "He says he wants to duel Romeo."

I nearly fell over. "A duel? As in a fight?"

"With sharp and pointed blades," said Mercutio. "Tybalt is angry with Romeo for breaking into the Capulet party last night and dancing with his cousin Juliet."

I wondered how mad Tybalt would be if he knew that Romeo was planning to *marry* his cousin Juliet?

It was almost funny.

But not quite.

"Tybalt is a master swordsman," said Mercutio. "I wouldn't want to tangle with him. If you see young Romeo before we do, tell him to see his father. He can give him the message."

Benvolio nodded. "Now come, Mercutio, let us leave this place. Devin, Frankie, be safe!"

The two men slid off into a side street and were gone.

"Devin, I feel very weird just now."

"Tell me about it," I said. "I think these tights are shrinking. My toes hurt way bad."

"Not that," she said. "I feel weird because we have this huge secret and can't tell anybody. I really don't want to take sides in this thing."

"I know what you mean," I said. "It's strange how we're totally in the middle. We're like the only friends of both Romeo and Juliet. Anyway, come on. Let's get this ladder to Juliet's house. It must be getting late."

We wandered once more through the narrow streets until we found ourselves in front of the Capulet mansion. By the smell of it, it was about lunchtime. I'm pretty sure I smelled those meatballs Italy is so famous for.

As we scurried around the back to the garden wall to test out the ladder, we found Juliet in her usual spot on the balcony. She looked like she was getting ready to do one of those long talking-to-herself speeches.

When no one was looking, Frankie tossed the ladder over the outer wall. We climbed over the top and into the garden, then flung the ladder up on to the balcony.

"Oh! Frankie! Devin!" said Juliet. "The clock struck nine when I sent the nurse, and she's not back yet!"

Frankie pulled herself up to the balcony. "Maybe she got lost? We did."

"Plus she's a slow walker," I said, coming up after.

"The messengers of love should be swift!" said Juliet, "not lumbering like an old mule. From nine till noon is three long hours! What if she never comes? Oh, I shall die on my balcony waiting forever for her—"

At that moment, the plodding steps of her nurse echoed up the inside stairs to her room. She came in huffing and puffing. "Oh, my, oh, dear—"

"Nurse!" cried Juliet, rushing to her. "What news do you bring?"

"Well, I—"

Juliet gasped. "You look sad. Is there sad news?"

"No, no . . ."

"Romeo does not love me?"

"It's not that. . . ."

"He is dead! Oh, my dear, dead Romeo—"

"Juliet!" shouted the nurse. "I'm tired! It makes my bones ache!" She huffed and puffed some more.

Juliet gave her a look. "I wish you had my bones and I had your news. Speak, good nurse, speak. Speak!"

"I can't speak!" she said. "I am too out of breath!"

I laughed. "How can you say you're out of breath when you have enough breath to say you're out of breath?"

The nurse gave me a piercing look. "Should you not fetch that rope ladder?"

"We already got it," I said. Then I buttoned my lip.

Meanwhile, Juliet was pacing faster and faster across the balcony. It was like watching a tennis game with only one player, who was rushing to hit the ball on both sides of the net. Finally, she stopped and stared at the nurse. "What does Romeo say of our marriage?"

"Oh, my head aches!" said the nurse.

"Romeo says his head aches?" said Juliet.

"If he heard this conversation he might," I whispered to Frankie. "Can't the nurse just come out with it?"

She chuckled. "Not according to the play. She keeps Juliet wondering for a long time."

"But what does Romeo say!" Juliet demanded finally.

The nurse took a deep breath. "Like an honest gentleman, and a courteous and kind and handsome gentleman, he says . . . wait . . . where is your mother?"

"Where is my mother?" Juliet repeated. "Why does Romeo want to know where my mother is? She's inside where she should be—what did Romeo say?"

The nurse breathed out heavily. "Well, then, now. He says to go to Friar Laurence's little cell, which is quite small and could use some tidying up, if you ask me—"

"Out with it, lady, or Devin and I will tell her!" Frankie yelled.

The nurse blinked. "Fine, then. Romeo says to go to Friar Laurence's cell this afternoon."

"And?"

"And Romeo will be there."

Juliet grunted. "And?"

"And . . . he'll be your husband and you will be his wife—"

"Yay!" shouted Frankie. "She got the message out!"

The nurse smiled. "Now, go test that ladder, so that later, Romeo can climb up to see his new bride. For now, Juliet, go must you quickly to the friar's cell—"

*Zoom!* Juliet was out of there in a flash.

The breeze from her leaving caused the book to flip to the next page. Thunder rumbled in the distance.

"What's going on?" I said.

Frankie glanced at the page. "Whoa! Hurry, Devin!"

"What?"

"Time passed. We'll miss the big wedding!"

She grabbed me by the arm and pulled me back down the rope ladder. We raced after Juliet through the streets, and around corners, following her pink heels.

"Man, can she run," I said, breathlessly.

"It's the love thing," added Frankie, huffing and puffing in her long dress.

As we raced through the gates, I caught sight of Benvolio and Mercutio again. It looked like they had too much lunch or something and it wasn't agreeing with them. Mercutio was looking especially sour.

"Keep going," said Frankie. "This scene doesn't involve them."

Just as we hurried out the gates, I heard the sharp sound of breaking glass.

"Frankie, I'm worried," I said, racing down the dusty road to Friar Laurence's place. "I mean, Romeo and Juliet getting together is nice and all, but all these guys with swords are really starting to bother me—"

"No time for that now—wedding—wedding!"

And it was.

By the time we spotted the little stone hut, Friar Laurence was in the garden holding the pair by the hands. "Ah, witnesses!" he said when he saw us.

"Witnesses to trouble brewing in town," I said.

"I think we'd better hurry this whole thing along."

"Yes," said Friar Laurence. He turned to Romeo and Juliet. "I, too, worry that we will be discovered."

"Friar, close our hands with holy words," said Romeo, gazing at Juliet. "Then death do what he will. It is enough that I may call her mine."

Death? I didn't like the sound of that. Frankie was frowning something awful, too. We both had a feeling something was going on in Verona, and it wasn't good.

Even as we stood there in the garden, the nice bright streaks of light that started the day were beginning to fade. Clouds were gathering on the distant horizon. And a strange wind whistled through the garden flowers.

"Frankie," I whispered, "what's going to happen?"

"I can't read ahead," she said, glancing at the page we were on. "The words are too blurry. And I don't think we should flip ahead. We'd miss the wedding."

I shuddered. "Okay. But I'm starting to be worried."

If something bad was brewing, Romeo and Juliet sure didn't notice. All they saw was themselves in love and wanting to get married.

The friar clasped their hands. "We'll make short work of this. Smile the heavens upon this holy act!"

I looked up at the heavens, but the clouds were

darkening by the minute, turning from gray to black when the friar finally took the two lovebirds into his cell.

"Frankie, I hate to say this, but I think Mr. Wexler was right. I have a feeling this story isn't going to end too well."

"But it's different now because we're here. Maybe we can make things turn out all right. Maybe we could give what might be a tragedy a happy ending."

"Cool. I like those much better," I said, managing to give her a grin. "All right, then, let's get back to town. I think the two lovebirds want some privacy."

But as we hurried back, Frankie and I realized that things in town were probably not going to be so lovey-dovey.

We were right.

# Chapter 10

We rushed through the gates and right away heard loud shouting coming from the main square where the play had started.

Mercutio, still looking like he had eaten too much lunch, was stumbling across the cobblestones away from Benvolio.

"Stay, Mercutio," said his friend. "Let's go home. The Capulets—"

"I don't care if it's Capulets!" snarled Mercutio.

"You should care," said Frankie. "Here comes Tybalt. And the look on his face is not at all about being friends."

"Too late," I said.

The Capulets were with us in an instant, led by

black-suited Tybalt himself. He gripped the handle of his sword, his eyes flashing. "Gentleman, a word with you!"

"Why not a word and a fight?" said Mercutio.

"Whoa, simmer down, Merc," I said. "We're all just walking here. Chill out, why don't you—"

Tybalt glared at Mercutio as if he couldn't hear me. "A fight? I'll give you one if you want one. You are a friend of Romeo, are you not?"

Benvolio stepped forward. "Let us go to some private place, or reason calmly, or else depart."

Mercutio stood his ground. "I will not budge."

"Wrong answer!" said Frankie. "Budging is, like, the perfect thing to be doing right about now. . . ."

"Besides," I added, "you've got lots of nice spots in this city. Why not go sight-seeing? I hear they make the best jumbo meatball grinders two streets over."

"Meatball?" said Tybalt. "Are you calling me a name, young sir?"

"Uh-oh," I whispered. "This isn't going well."

Tybalt sneered. "And so! Here comes Romeo."

We all turned.

Romeo came skipping into the square, looked at himself in the fountain, and smiled at his reflection.

I nudged Frankie. "Oh, man! Nobody knows it, but he just married Juliet."

Frankie nodded slowly, her eyes fixed on Romeo. "Which makes him . . . Tybalt's cousin."

Romeo kept grinning into the water. Finally, lifting his head up and seeing us all watching him, he came bounding over as if he were a puppy just called for his supper. "Tybalt!" he said.

"Romeo!" Tybalt snarled. "Thou art a villain!"

Romeo stopped, but held on to his smile. "Tybalt, the reason that I have to love thee excuses my rage at such a greeting. Therefore, farewell—"

Tybalt stepped in his way. "Boy, this shall not excuse the injuries that thou hast done me. Therefore, turn and draw your sword."

Romeo froze. "I never injured thee, Tybalt. I love thee better than thou canst understand. And so, good Capulet, whose name I hold as dearly as my own, I go . . . ."

Romeo turned once more to walk away.

"What, Romeo?" snapped Mercutio. "Will you let your enemy go by? Tybalt, will you just walk away?"

Tybalt turned to Mercutio, his hand on his sword.

The sliding of Mercutio's sword from its sheath happened so fast that Frankie and I barely had a chance to step back. Tybalt's sword was out even faster.

Romeo shouted. "Put down your swords. Stop this!"

"Or use plastic ones!" I said. "They bend really easy!"

But Mercutio and Tybalt were already at it, clashing their very real, very metal blades together.

*Clank! Cling!* The air was silver with swords.

Romeo rushed into the mess to try to part the two. "Gentlemen, stop this now. The prince hath forbid fighting in the streets. Hold off, Tybalt. Stop, Mercutio—"

But even as Romeo stepped between them, holding his arms high to stop them, Tybalt lunged at Mercutio, whipping his sword right under Romeo's arm.

"Ahhh!" cried Mercutio, as the blade struck him.

Frankie screamed. I jumped back, pulling her with me. "Pointed swords!" I screamed. "Get us out of here!"

But it was too late, Mercutio stumbled back against Benvolio, clutching his side. Tybalt's gang pulled him away.

"I'm hurt," growled Mercutio, sinking to the ground.

We all crowded around him. Benvolio knelt next to him. "How bad is the wound?"

"Just a scratch," said Mercutio. "A scratch. But 'tis enough." His face tightened, and the smirk left his lips.

"Someone get a doctor!" said Frankie. "Is it bad?"

"No," said Mercutio. "Not too bad. 'Tis not so deep as a well, nor so wide as a church door, but 'tis enough. It will do. I am dying—oh! Montagues and

Capulets! A plague on both your houses! Romeo, why did you come between us? I was hurt under your arm!"

"I thought I could stop you both," Romeo said.

"You stopped only me. And Tybalt stopped his sword in my side!" Mercutio said, trying to make a joke.

We pulled him to the fountain and gave him some water to drink. He sipped a bit, then cried out again, "A plague on both your houses! Benvolio, take me inside or I'll faint—"

Benvolio and some others picked him up and carried him into the nearest house. Romeo stood staring at the cobblestones at his feet. "He's hurt for me. I did this."

"Hey," I said, "you tried to stop it."

"It's Tybalt's fault for stabbing him when you tried to pull them apart. He cheated," said Frankie.

"Tybalt," said Romeo. "Since I'm married to his cousin Juliet, he's my cousin, too. For only an hour, he's been my cousin. Yet, he does not know."

Breathing heavily, his face red, Benvolio came out of the house where they carried Mercutio. "Oh, Romeo, Romeo, brave Mercutio is dead. But watch! Here comes the furious Tybalt back again—"

Romeo whirled on his heels. "Not as furious as I!" he snapped. "Tybalt, you villain! You took Mercutio.

Now either thou or I, or both, must go with him!"

Tybalt swung his sword at Romeo. "Thou wretched boy, thou shalt follow thy cousin!"

"No!" cried Frankie. "Will you guys stop this!"

But the two fighters leaped at each other, clashing and clanging their swords across the square and into the marketplace.

"Dumb fighting!" I said. "This stinks!"

Frankie and I tried to help Romeo, since he was the star of the show, but Tybalt's gang started getting into the act, too. We tumbled some baskets on them, because we knew they weren't supposed to be in the scene. They threw fruits and vegetables at us, because they probably figured the same thing about us.

But in the spotlight were Tybalt and Romeo. They fought their way around the fountain. *Clank! Pling!*

Once, Romeo even splashed through the fountain, but Tybalt was ready for him. It was like a movie swordfight. They were all over the square, even going up the stairs of one house, across an alley, and down the other side, clashing blades all the way.

Romeo, even though he was, like, Mr. Married Man, fought amazingly well, getting in some good swats against Tybalt, who was the great swordsman.

It was clear that Romeo didn't really want to hurt the guy. I mean, after all, they were related.

Finally, Tybalt did this fancy twirl to give Romeo a

final lunge, but lost his balance, fell, and slid sideways onto Romeo's sword.

"Ahh!" he moaned, and dropped to the cobblestones. Then he shuddered, groaned loudly, and went still.

It was over in a moment. His friends rushed to him, but he didn't say much.

Tybalt was already gone. Lifeless. Dead.

"Oh, my gosh!" said Frankie. "I can't believe this."

Benvolio dashed over to us. "Frankie, Devin, take Romeo away. He knows not what he has done." He waved his hand in front of Romeo's glazed eyes. "Romeo, away with you, be gone. The prince will sentence you to death if you are captured. Begone—"

Dazed, Romeo stumbled backward, his eyes still fixed on Tybalt's lifeless form.

"Oh!" he cried suddenly. "I am fortune's fool!"

The tramping feet of soldiers thundered into the square.

"Go!" yelled Benvolio. "The prince's guard is here!"

To escape, we had to scurry up a set of stairs to the overhanging rooftops, practically dragging the dazed Romeo behind us.

From above we watched a crowd filling the square, including Mr. and Mrs. Montague, the Capulets, and finally the prince.

The prince called for witnesses, and Benvolio, held by the guards, told him what had happened.

"Tybalt killed Mercutio," he said, "and Romeo, trying to keep the peace, was forced by Tybalt to fight. They went at it like lightning, and before I could draw them apart, Tybalt fell, and Romeo fled."

Mrs. Capulet shook her head. "This man is a friend of Romeo. He speaks not true. Romeo slew Tybalt. Romeo must not live!"

"No, no," said old Montague. "Tybalt killed Mercutio, and Romeo merely did what the prince himself would have done—"

The prince held up his hand, then stood silent for a while. "Tybalt was a killer, and Romeo did kill a killer. For that offense, we exile him from fair Verona under penalty of death. Let Romeo leave now! For when he's found, that hour is his last!"

"Frankie, this isn't good," I whispered from our roof.

"No kidding," she said. "Let's get Romeo out of here and tell Juliet right away. She needs to know."

We tugged poor Romeo across the rooftops to Friar Laurence's cell, then shot back to the streets, to tell Juliet the very, very, very bad news.

# Chapter 11

*Whoomf!* We threw the rope ladder up.

"You know, Frankie," I said. "This ladder was supposed to sneak Romeo into Juliet's house so they could be together."

"Yeah," she said, hauling herself up the dangling ladder. "It doesn't look like that's going to happen anytime soon."

We pulled ourselves up on to the balcony. I peered in. Juliet was all goopy-eyed and sighing and giggling.

"Poor kid," I whispered. "She doesn't have a clue what just happened."

But even as we watched, the nurse came bustling in. "Oh, it's terrible!" she cried. "Tybalt slain! And Romeo, oh!"

Juliet bolted up from the bed. "Tybalt slain! And Romeo—what? Slain also? Then I shall slay myself—"

"Hold on!" I said, climbing over the balcony and bursting into the room. "Did anybody ever mention that you two don't really communicate too well? Look, here's the situation. First Tybalt killed Mercutio, then Romeo killed Tybalt. Not that he wanted to. He tried to stop all the fighting. But Tybalt wouldn't let it go."

"My husband has killed my cousin?" said Juliet.

"That's about the size of it," said Frankie. "And now Romeo has to beat it out of town before the prince's guards—or any Capulets—find him."

Juliet staggered on her feet. "Then . . . is this the end?"

Frankie held up the book. "No. A little over halfway."

"Which means that we still have a chance to make this end good," I said. "I think we can. I hope we can."

"I must see Romeo," said Juliet. "I must see him!"

Frankie breathed in, then glanced at me. "Hmmm. I wonder. Maybe Friar Laurence can come up with a plan. And Romeo can swing by and tell you what we've figured out. I mean, this will be the last place anyone would look for him."

"Plus," I said, "after all the trouble we've been to, he's got to use that rope ladder at least once!"

"Absolutely," said Frankie.

"Nurse, go to Romeo," said Juliet. "Find him and give him this ring." She pushed a ring into the nurse's hand. "And bid him come to take his last farewell."

"I will do it!" said the nurse. She scurried out and down the stairs.

"And we'd better leave the other way," I said. Then, I turned to Juliet one more time. "Cheer up, Jules. Friar Laurence seems like a smart guy. If anyone can think of a plan, he can."

She looked at me, but said nothing.

As we scuttled down the ladder, Frankie sighed. "Devin, things are bad," she said. "Very, very bad."

"Hey, I know. I hate to see her like that."

"Yeah. Me, too."

When we jumped down to the garden, Mr. and Mrs. Capulet were just returning from the square and were walking in one of the hallways inside with a young man.

"We've seen him before," I said.

Frankie peered closer. "It's that guy Paris. The one who wanted to marry Juliet. I wonder what he wants."

I grinned. "There's only one way to find out." I pointed at an open window nearby. "We creep in and listen. One thing I've learned from this Shakespeare guy. He doesn't put in dumb stuff. If this is a scene in the play, there's got to be a reason. I say we go into major snoopy spy mode and listen in."

Frankie began to nod. "It's ideas like that that make me glad we're in this together. Let's do it."

Making myself as skinny as possible, I slipped through the window and dropped to the floor. I opened it some more for Frankie and her dress to slide in. Then we crept around and into the hallway, just as the Capulets and Paris were coming our way.

"The rug on the wall," I whispered. "Let's hide behind it."

"We better hide good," she whispered, as we darted behind a large tapestry. "If they find us, all they have to do is shout and all those nasty-looking guards will charge from the street with their swords and beards and torches and we're done for! And maybe the prince will do more than banish us."

"Like maybe . . . *vanish* us?"

"Maybe. Shhh—"

"I haven't had the time to talk to my daughter," Mr. Capulet was saying. "Juliet dearly loved her cousin Tybalt. So did I. We are all confused and saddened by his death."

Paris spoke. "It's only that, well, I love her and I would marry her to stop her grieving. . . ."

"Sorry, pal!" I whispered. "An hour too late for that."

"But I understand, sir," Paris added. "I bid you good night."

He turned and walked away from Capulet, heading down the hallway past us, and toward the garden.

I peered out my end of the tapestry to see him leave, but what I saw instead sent shivers up my spine.

Beyond the door at the end of the hallway leading into the garden was the nurse.

She hustled across the grass, stopped, looked both ways, then waved to the bushes. Which I thought was odd. Until the bushes parted, and out came none other than Romeo himself, dashing across the open garden to the ladder.

"Oh, my gosh!" I gasped. "No, no—"

"Paris is going to spot Romeo!" Frankie said. "He's going to see him! What are we going to do—"

Old Capulet turned on his heels. "Paris, wait!"

The instant before Romeo passed before the doorway, Paris turned around. "Yes, my lord?"

Romeo flitted by outside. I could breathe again.

"I have thought this over, my son. We are all in grief about noble Tybalt's death. But your love of our daughter may help dry her tears—"

"It's Romeo she's crying over!" whispered Frankie.

"My lord?" said Paris. "What are you saying?"

"That you should marry her!" said Capulet,

almost laughing. "Yes, and Juliet will obey me in this. Yes! I like the idea. Dear wife, go now to Juliet and tell her that on Wednesday next . . . wait, what day is it today?"

"Monday, my lord," said Paris.

"Monday? Well then, Wednesday is too soon—"

"Or too late," I whispered.

"Thursday, then?" said Mrs. Capulet.

"Yes, Thursday," said the old man. "Dear wife, tell Juliet that on Thursday she shall be married to this noble gentleman Paris!"

Frankie and I nearly choked. But it would have given us away. But, come on! Juliet can't have *two* husbands! *That* would never work!

Of course, Paris thought it would work just fine. In fact, the guy leaped for joy just like the first time.

"Oh, I wish Thursday were tomorrow!" he cried.

Capulet laughed. "Well, good," he said. "Thursday be it then. Wife, prepare Juliet for her wedding day!"

Capulet and Paris walked off into the main part of the house, while Mrs. Capulet walked toward the stairs to Juliet's room.

"Holy cow!" I said. "Romeo's up there! She'll catch him. The guards will come rushing in! The prince will find out! We have to save him! I have an idea."

I slipped out from behind the rug in full view of everyone.

"Devin!" hissed Frankie, still hiding. "What are you doing?"

"Stalling her," I said. "Oh, lady Capulet?"

She stopped on the stairs and turned. "Yes?"

"Did you know that—that—that—"

I completely went blank. It was probably because I didn't have the book. It was with Frankie.

"Well?" Mrs. Capulet said, stepping down one step.

Finally, an idea came to me. "There's someone . . . locked in the bathroom!"

"The what?"

"The bathroom! Quick! This way!"

I ran to the stairs and pulled Lady Capulet down into the main room. Then I opened the nearest door and pushed her through. I shut the door behind her, and put a small table in front of it. Immediately, she started banging on the door with her fists.

Frankie rushed over. "Devin, this is totally nutty. She's not liking it. And by the way, did they even have bathrooms four hundred years ago?"

I looked at my friend. "All I can say is, if they didn't—eeeww! Come on!"

We hightailed it up the stairs as fast as we could go, but something weird was happening. It was like we were moving in slow motion, while time was passing quickly.

The light was changing. The torches along the stairway walls burnt down and went out as we passed them.

"Whoa—Frankie!" I said. "The scene must be changing!"

"I know!" she said. "Time . . . is . . . passing!"

By the time things were normal again and we blasted into Juliet's room, it was practically morning.

And Romeo and Juliet were holding hands, looking out over the balcony at the sky.

# Chapter 12

I rushed in. "Hey! Guys!" I said.

But they didn't even hear me. They only heard and saw each other. It's like they were totally focused on themselves. It was romantic, I guess, but also slightly icky.

"It's nearly daylight," said Frankie. "Romeo, you have to leave—"

Romeo, still keeping his eyes locked on Juliet's, said, "It's nearly daylight. . . ."

"This is what I'm saying!" said Frankie.

Paying no attention to us, Romeo said, "Juliet, I must go to Mantua. Friar Laurence has arranged a place for me to stay. I must be gone and live, or stay and die. But I am content, so long as I am with you."

Juliet laughed. "That light is not daylight," she

said. "It is some meteor that the sun exhaled to be to thee this night a torch bearer and light thee on thy way to Mantua. Therefore stay. . . ."

I shook my head. "Boy, for being in mortal danger, they sure talk fancy."

"Hey, you two!" said Frankie. "Alert! Knock, knock!"

Juliet tore her eyes away from Romeo for a fraction of a second, then seemed startled. "Devin! Frankie! I am sorry. We did not see you—"

I laughed. "No kidding. You guys haven't taken your eyes off each other since we got here."

"Yeah, look," added Frankie. "We're sorry to bust up your love-fest, but any minute now Juliet's mom is probably going to get out of the closet that Devin locked her in, and fly in here to give you some very bad news."

"We stalled her as long as we could," I said. "But things are moving really fast now, so I think it's exit time for Romeo. Down the ladder, pal."

For the first time since the play began, Romeo looked as if he understood the danger he was in. "What is the bad news?"

"First things first," said Frankie. "We need to get you out of here pronto—"

At that very moment, heels clacked down the hall.

"I would know those footsteps anywhere!" said Juliet. "It is my mother!"

Romeo turned to her. "One kiss and I'll descend."

"I must hear from thee every day in the hour," said Juliet, giving him actually a couple of kisses.

*Clack! Clack!* More footsteps. And closer!

"Excuse me! Pay attention! Hello! Mrs. Mom is nearly here!" snapped Frankie.

"And ten to one, she's very, very mad!" I said.

Romeo slid over the balcony and began to climb down the all-important rope ladder. We looked down at him as he jumped into the dirt of the garden.

"Oh!" gasped Juliet. "Now thou art so low as one dead in the bottom of a tomb!"

"Nice, cheery thought," I muttered.

"Good-bye, until later, then," said Romeo from below.

He fled across the garden and hopped over the wall, just as the door flew open and Juliet's mom barged in, all snarly. And, of course, Frankie and I had to dodge her. So we slipped over the balcony and hung there, listening to the whole scene.

And it wasn't good. It was bad. Very, very bad.

"I have splendid news for you, Juliet. On Thursday, the gallant nobleman Paris will make thee his joyful bride!"

Juliet rocked on her feet a little. "I wonder at this haste. Tell my father I will not marry yet, and when I do I swear it shall be Romeo, whom you know I hate, rather than Paris—"

"What!" boomed a voice in the hallway. The door burst open and Mr. Capulet himself barged in, huffing and puffing as if he ran all the way up the stairs. "What is this? You'll be in church on Thursday and marry Paris—or never look me in the face again!"

Juliet's eyes bugged out. It was terrible to hear a dad say that. She opened her mouth to respond, but he raised his hand sharply.

"Reply not!" he shouted. "Do not answer me! I am a cursed father to have such a child!"

"That is *so* not fair," Frankie whispered.

But her father wasn't quite done. "Juliet, you shall marry Paris—or live no longer in my house! Live on the streets, if you like, but I shall have no daughter!"

We all watched as he stormed from the room, Juliet's mother with him.

The nurse, who was cowering in the hallway, came in. So did we.

"Dear girl," said the nurse, "I heard it all."

"What will I do?" asked Juliet. "I already have a husband. But I cannot tell them that. I cannot tell anyone!"

The nurse breathed deeply. "Oh, dear girl," she said. "Romeo is banished. You may never see him again. I think it best you marry Paris. . . ."

"What?" I hissed. "That's crazy talk. This is called *Romeo and Juliet*, not *Paris and Juliet*. That doesn't even sound right."

"This second match excels your first," the nurse went on, ignoring me.

I think Juliet was flabbergasted to hear her old nurse say this. She was quiet for a while, leaning over the balcony toward us. Finally, she turned, with what I thought was a ghost of an idea in her eyes.

"Very well," she said. "Tell my mother that I shall go to Friar Laurence to pray for forgiveness for displeasing my father."

"This is wisely done," said the nurse. She got up and quietly left the room.

Juliet stood for a moment on the balcony. Where tears had filled her eyes, there was another expression now.

"Wait a sec," said Frankie. "You're not really thinking of marrying Paris?"

She shook her head. "I'll to the friar to know his remedy. If all else fails, I will myself have power to die."

"Let's hope it doesn't come to that!" said Frankie. "Come on. Friar Laurence will know what to do."

"All right!" I cheered. "The big scheme to make everything right! Do you think it really can work out?"

Frankie looked at the book. With lots of doubt in her eyes, she said, "I sure hope so. Let's go."

A fraction of a second later, we went.

All the way into the next scene.

# Chapter 13

Friar Laurence was pacing the floor of his little cell as usual. And since it was such a small room, he really only did a half-pace before he ran out of cell and had to turn around again.

"Bad news, friar guy!" I said, when Frankie, Juliet, and I crowded in.

"No need to tell me, Devin," said the friar. "Paris has just been here. He told me how on Thursday Juliet is to be married to him."

"Man, the dude moves fast!" I said.

"I will not marry him!" said Juliet. "Never!"

"Cool down, Jules," said Frankie. "Friar—"

"Friar," said Juliet, her eyes flashing, "prevent this, or I'll find my own way to stop it. By stopping my heart from beating! I'll do it!" She pulled out a dagger.

"Where'd you get that thing!" I gasped.

"No!" Friar Laurence grabbed the pointy object from her and tossed it away. "Hold, daughter!"

"Then, bid me leap off the highest tower in Verona—"

The friar clucked his tongue. "Oh, dear, no, no . . ."

"Or chain me with bears!" she said.

"Are there bears in Verona?" I asked, looking around.

"Child, do not say such things," said the friar.

"Then I shall jump into the river and be eaten by a serpent! If that doesn't work, I shall—"

"Whoa, dudette!" I said. "This is very uncool talk. Think happy thoughts. There's always a way out."

"That's right," said Frankie. "Just calm down, Jules. Maybe the friar has a plan to turn all this around."

It seemed like he did. The friar scuttled over to a high shelf on the wall and slid off a tiny glass bottle. "Behold!"

"You're going to hide her in that?" I asked. "She seems too big—"

"No, no!" he said, giving me the eye. He bent over to a small wooden cabinet and pulled out a larger bottle. Inside it was some kind of purplish liquid. He poured some from the big bottle into the little bottle.

"Well, then, Juliet," he said quietly. "Go home, be merry, and give consent to marry Paris."

I frowned. "That's the plan? Maybe we weren't clear about something. Juliet *doesn't* want to marry Paris."

Frankie nodded. "This isn't quite the sort of plan we were thinking of—"

"I have not finished!" scowled the friar. "Wednesday is tomorrow. Tomorrow night, Juliet, drink this at bedtime."

He held out the tiny bottle.

"What will happen?" asked Frankie.

The friar smiled. "A single taste of this, dear Juliet, and you will have no warmth, no breath, the roses in thy lips and cheeks shall fade, your body shall be stiff and stark and cold. . . ."

"That's sort of the definition of, you know . . . *death*," Frankie said.

"Juliet will fall into a sleep that looks like, but is not, death," said the friar.

"You're sure about that 'is not' part?" I said.

"Quite sure," he said. "And in this *seeming* death Juliet shall be for two and forty hours, then awake as from a pleasant sleep."

"And the waking up part," I said. "Is that guaranteed?"

"Oh, yes!" said the friar. "I tried it once myself. But there is one thing—"

"Here it comes," I said. "There's always a catch."

"When Thursday comes," said the friar, "everyone will think you have died. You will then be taken to the ancient Capulet tomb."

Juliet gulped. "And what about Romeo?"

"Phase two of the plan?" I said, looking at the friar. "We call Romeo up and he shoots back from Mantua?"

"Exactly," said the friar. "A friend of mine will take a letter to Romeo that will tell him of our plan. Your husband shall come back here in the dead of night and he and I together will be in the tomb when you awake."

"Oh, I get it," I said. "And then—*poof!* Romeo will whisk you off to a honeymoon in Mantua, and you'll live happily ever after, fun in the sun and all that? Right, Frankie?"

She glanced at the book. "The words are blurry, but, yeah, that's the plan."

I cheered up a little bit. It always helps to have a plan when the situation seems really, really bad. "I feel good about this. I think it will work. I really do."

Juliet seemed more cheerful, too. "I shall do it!" she said, a sound of hope in her voice for the first time in quite a while.

"So," said Frankie. "No more thoughts of being lunch for river serpents?"

Juliet laughed. "No!"

"Be strong and prosperous!" said Friar Laurence. "I'll send a friar with speed to Mantua with my letters to thy Lord."

With no more chatter, we left the little cell and made our way back to Juliet's house to put our plan into action.

# Chapter 14

When we got to the street in front of the Capulet house, we stopped. Inside, the place was bustling and buzzing and all about the upcoming wedding.

Caterers were everywhere, balancing loaded trays and moving chunky old wooden chairs.

And in the center of it all was Mr. Capulet, barking orders. "More napkins there! More torches there!"

It was definitely going to be a big bash.

Juliet groaned and started to shake. "Oh, no . . ."

"Hey, don't worry," Frankie whispered to her. "Our plan will work like clockwork. You gotta have faith."

It was then that Mr. Capulet boomed out something that stopped us cold.

"Hurry, with the candles there!" he shouted to a

bunch of candle-carrying guys. "Our wedding is not Thursday—it shall be tomorrow. I have changed my mind! The wedding shall be tomorrow morning!"

The three of us stared at one another.

"It's hopeless, hopeless!" said Juliet. She buried her face in her hands, rushed into the house, and up the stairs to her room.

"We'll be hiding in the garden if you need us!" I called. Then I turned to Frankie. "Holy cow. Is this going to mess up Friar Laurence's big plan or what?"

"If the friar's letter doesn't get to Romeo in time, of course, it will mess it up!" said Frankie. "And if we're stuck here watching Juliet, we can't tell Romeo about the change in plans. We can't be in two places at once. . . ."

All of a sudden, she stopped. She pulled the book from her pocket and stared at it. Suddenly, we were both thinking the same thing. And it was radical.

"Wait a second . . . you're not thinking—" I started.

But she was way ahead of me. "I *am* thinking, Devin. And I'm thinking it's the only way. The only way to help these guys is to be in two places at once. Devin, we need to split up."

"That's risky, very risky. Plus, it's a bit too much like what's going on with the lovebirds. Splitting up is bad."

"I know," she said. "But if I go to Mantua to some scene with Romeo in it and you stay here to see that nothing bad happens to Juliet, just maybe we can pull this off. Devin, like they say in all the junky action movies ever made . . . *it's up to us!*"

"I love that line!" I said. "Hey, if there's no other way . . ."

"I don't see one," she said.

"Then let's do it!"

Frankie nodded. She took the book and held it open to the page we were on. "Okay, here we are in act four, scene two. If I can find the very next scene with Romeo in it, and explain to him what's going on . . ."

"Sounds good," I said. "But we'd better stand apart so that I stay here."

"Brace yourself!" I said. "I hope we meet up later."

"Well—yeah!"

Frankie moved off to the far side of the street. She gave me a little wave, then started flipping the pages, one by one.

*Kkkkk!* Lightning flashed right over the Capulets' roof.

"That is not a good thing!" boomed the old man from inside. "I fear some evil will cloud our festival!"

It wasn't evil. It was just Frankie.

She flipped another page.

*Kkkk!* More lightning, closer this time.

Then, before you could say Romeo five times fast, the sky went black, and a dark V-shaped rip appeared across the sky, as if we were on a page being torn in half.

With each page Frankie turned, more thunder boomed. Lightning flashed. Suddenly—*Oooof!*—I was thrown hard to the street. Frankie tumbled, too, just as a deep peal of thunder rolled overhead—*boo-ooom!*

"Frankie!" I yelled. But already she was being pulled away from me on the other side of the black rip.

"Devin!" she shouted.

But an instant later—*kkkk!*—Frankie was gone.

The lightning faded. And I was alone on the street.

"Good luck, pal," I said, as the last of the lightning bolts flashed across the sky. "And for me, too!"

I hurried into Juliet's garden. Hours had obviously passed, and now it was night, the night before the wedding. Voices were coming from Juliet's room.

I was worried. I never liked the idea of Juliet taking stuff that the old friar cooked up in that little cell of his.

Quickly, I climbed up the rope ladder and peeked up over the balcony railing. The nurse and Juliet's mother were setting out a fancy wedding dress, all frilly and long with silver sparkles and puffy sleeves.

"Thank you," said Juliet. "Let me now be left alone."

"Get thee to bed, and rest, Juliet," said her mother softly.

"Farewell, Mother," said Juliet. "Farewell, nurse."

I could tell from the way Juliet said it, that she meant it to sound casual, but it was probably final. The others didn't pick up on it, but I knew that if all worked out the way the friar had planned, she would be off to Mantua in a day or so, and it might be a long time before she saw her mother and nurse again.

"God knows when we shall meet again," Juliet whispered as they left, and it made me think of Frankie.

I didn't like being split up from my best friend in a story that was about two people being split up. It scared me.

Juliet stood at the door where her mother had just gone, and stayed there for a long time.

"Fear runs through my veins," she murmured softly.

"Mine, too," I said, climbing into the room. "But we should look on the bright side—"

*Kkkk!* Lightning crackled in the distant sky to the south. I wondered if Mantua was that way and if Frankie had found Romeo. I hoped she was okay.

"What if this medicine does not work?" said Juliet. "Shall I be married to Paris?"

"I don't think that will happen."

"But what if I am laid in the tomb and wake before Romeo comes for me? What if I cannot breathe in the tomb . . . ?"

"Don't go there," I said. "Things will be okay, I'm pretty sure."

She shivered, as lightning crackled again in the south.

I thought again about Frankie all alone in that strange city. When I focused again, Juliet was carefully and calmly taking that small bottle from the folds of her dress. She pulled out the tiny cork in the top.

She gave me a look, then held it to her lips. "Romeo! I drink to thee!"

I held my breath as she swallowed the purple stuff in a single swig. She stood still for a second, then fell back upon her bed. The curtains tumbled down from their ties and fell closed around her.

"Oh, man!" I whispered. "You actually did it!"

It was then that I noticed that time seemed to be passing quickly. Frankie, wherever she was, was definitely reading ahead. The distant lightning never really stopped. Every few minutes it crackled and flashed across the sky. Deep, dark night came on and then the sky began to grow lighter.

I felt helpless. I wanted to help Juliet. I wanted to get to Frankie. But without the book, there was nothing I could do.

"Frankie," I said, looking in the direction of Mantua, "I hope you find Romeo quick. The clock is ticking!"

Then, I heard noises in the house below. It was the sound of pots and pans clanking together. I knew then that all kinds of cooking and baking were underway.

The wedding party—short one bride—had begun.

# Chapter 15

"Fetch the logs!" old Mr. Capulet boomed out in his gruff voice. "Start the fires, so that our festive house be warm on this wedding day. And start the music there!"

I stood near Juliet's bed. "It's going to be rough on him and your mom," I said, in my own sort of soliloquy. "They're going to think you're . . . well, you know."

I didn't even want to say it myself.

Funny-sounding music, probably from the same band that played at the masked ball where Romeo and Juliet first met, began to play the Verona top forty.

"Nurse!" Mr. Capulet called from downstairs. "Go

wake Juliet. Tell her that her bridegroom, noble Paris, has come already. Go!"

I heard the nurse bustle her way up the stairs to Juliet's room. I knew what would happen. I stepped back to the balcony and hid just outside the room.

"Juliet!" the nurse called cheerily from the hall. "I must wake you! Your wedding day! Everyone's waiting!"

The door flew open and the nurse bounded in, carrying a candle and setting it on a table near Juliet's bed. The bed curtains were still drawn around the girl.

"Oh, still asleep?" the nurse said with a chuckle. She carefully pulled the curtains aside and peeked in. "You sleepyhead, wake up. What? No word for me?"

She leaned closer. It was hard to watch, but I couldn't look away. "Sweetheart," she said, "my dear, wake up . . . come now . . ." She took Juliet by the hand and patted it. A shudder went through her large frame, and she pulled her own hands away.

"Cold," she said. "Cold. Alas, alas, help, help! My lady's . . . dead!" She shrieked it over and over. "My lady's dead! Dead! Dead!"

*Blam!* The door blasted open and Juliet's mom raced in. "What noise is this? What are you saying!"

"Look, look! Oh, heavy day!" cried the nurse, her hands hovering around Juliet, but not daring to touch her again.

Mrs. Capulet pushed the nurse away and gently tried to shake Juliet awake. "Juliet . . . Juliet . . . Oh me, oh me . . ." She nearly fell from the bed. "My child! My only life, revive, look up, or I will die with thee. Help, help! Call help—"

I got this huge lump in my throat and tears started to fill up in my eyes. Man, I so wanted to tell them that Juliet was only sleeping, but I couldn't. If everyone knew, the whole plan would go up in smoke.

And that would be a real tragedy.

Now Mr. Capulet staggered in, his face gray, his mouth hanging open. Others in the house followed him, crowding around the bed and shouting and crying over Juliet. It was too painful to watch.

"She's dead, she's dead, she's dead!" her mother wailed.

Her father leaned close. "Oh, oh . . . she's cold. Her joints are stiff. Death lies on her like a frost upon the sweetest flower of all the field!"

More and more people gathered around Juliet. Finally, Friar Laurence himself was ushered in, along with poor Paris. They seemed surprised by all the commotion.

"Come," said the friar, "is the bride ready to go to church?"

Her father stole a look at the friar, his eyes flashing. "Ready to go, but never to return. Oh, Paris, the night before thy wedding day, Death came for thy wife!"

Paris staggered back from the bed, bursting into tears now, too. "How I longed to see this face, but now I see so terrible a sight!"

"Oh, unhappy day!" howled Mrs. Capulet. "Cursed, wretched, hateful day!"

They all collapsed around the bed. Friar Laurence knew it was all going according to plan, but even he seemed sick at the idea of putting these people through this. He got them to leave the room. "Peace now, she is gone. In her best gown let us take her to church now, and then the tomb."

Mr. Capulet took a deep breath and nodded slowly. "All happy things we ordered for the wedding feast, now furnish us the blackest funeral. Her bridal flowers now will decorate her tomb."

One by one, they all left, leaving only the friar in the room with Juliet. I hopped in from the balcony.

"Is she really okay?" I said.

He turned to me. "Ah, Devin. Things go well, for the moment. Juliet shall soon be taken for her peaceful sleep in the tomb. It shall not be long now. I dearly hope Romeo will get my letters in time . . . I hope . . . I hope. . . ."

Even as he said this, the distant storm seemed to

get louder. Lightning flashed across the morning sky, and thick clouds darkened the horizon.

"The skies themselves seem to speak of what happens here," he said. "The heavens know our plan."

I stepped out onto the balcony and looked up. Black clouds swirled where just the day before bright sun had shown. I knew what was going on.

It was a storm all right.

Only the storm wasn't a natural one.

It was Frankie.

At that moment—*kkkk!*—a bolt of bright white light shot across the sky and exploded over the house.

"Holy cow!" I cried, stepping back. Not quickly enough. Another bolt came flying in from nowhere—*kkkk!*—and I was sent hurtling off the balcony.

But I didn't hurtle through the plants and bushes and into the garden. I kept tumbling and bouncing until I landed on something hard. It was a street.

And Friar Laurence wasn't next to me.

Frankie was.

# Chapter 16

"Am I glad to see you!" I cried, leaping to my feet. The storm had stopped. I looked around at a square with a bubbling fountain. "Where are we?"

"We're in Mantua," said Frankie, dusting herself off and tucking the book into her dress again. "But we could be on the moon, for all the difference it makes."

I shook my head to clear it. "What do you mean? Did you tell Romeo the plan?"

"Tell him the plan?" she snapped. "I haven't even found the guy! I spent the entire time just getting to this point here! First, I flipped too far ahead, then I flipped back. When I finally wound up here, the Mantuan guards chased me all around because I had come from Verona and they thought I was carrying the plague or something."

"The plague?" I said. "Why would you carry one of those around?"

She shrugged. "From the way they talked, it's some kind of bad disease."

"Eew."

"No kidding," she said. "Me, in my nice purple gown made by PTA moms, carrying something icky? As if. Anyway, they said that if I came from Verona, I must have passed through some sick villages between there and here. They were going to turn me back—but, of course, I did the old flipperoo and—"

"Wait!" I said. "Something just clicked in my head."

"I hope it was your brain turning on, because mine has just about had it."

"It was," I said. "Listen, Frankie. If the guards were turning back all the people from Verona, it means that Romeo probably never got the letter from Friar Laurence's messenger. I mean, they don't have E-mail, right? So it's regular old-fashioned snail mail. And if it came from Verona—*fwit!*—back it goes!"

She blinked. "Whoa, Dev, you're right!"

"That's the second time in, like, a day. Pretty cool."

"Cool, yeah, but it means we have to find Romeo

pronto, or he won't get the message at all, and the plan goes up like a burger left too long on the grill."

I took a moment to think about burgers before getting back to the issue at hand. "Okay, maybe we should just try yelling real loud. Romeo's gotta appear in this scene sooner or later. When he does, we tell him the deal, swing by Verona, beep twice, Juliet scampers out of the tomb, they zoom off on their honeymoon, and everybody lives happily ever after!"

Frankie looked at me. "You know, Devin, I'd really like the story to end that way. Let's make it happen."

"We'll give it our best shot! Romeo! Hey, Romeo!"

Frankie, because she had been doing most of the reading, had been sort of stung by the Shakespeare bug. "Romeo!" she called out. "Romeo, Romeo, where art thou, Romeo!"

That's when we heard it.

"You there!"

The voice came from a nearby doorway. We spotted a young man just stepping into the street. "Dost thou seek Romeo of Verona?"

I gasped. "Frankie, he's talking Shakespeare!"

"Yes!" Frankie said to the man. "We do seek Romeo!"

"We need to tell him something," I added.

He nodded. "If you speak of Juliet, I already told him that her body sleeps in the Capulet tomb—"

"So he *knows* the plan! This is great!" I cheered.

"—and that her soul now rests with the angels," the guy finished.

I stopped cheering. "Wait. Say that last part again?"

"I was in Verona to see dear Juliet laid in the Capulet vault. I came here at once to tell Romeo that his beloved Juliet is dead."

I staggered back. Frankie staggered forward. Between us, there was a whole lot of staggering going on.

"WHAT!" I shouted. "Dead? Dead! You told him Juliet is dead!"

"Of course!" the guy said.

"But she's not dead!" I practically shrieked. "She's just pretending with a sleeping potion that Friar Laurence gave her! We have to tell Romeo the truth before he does something dumb! How did he take the news?"

"He was sad. If I remember correctly, he said something like, 'my life is over.' Maybe not exactly those words, but something like that. . . ."

"WHERE IS HE?" Frankie shouted at him

The guy's forehead wrinkled and he scratched his chin. "He was going to . . . going to . . . someplace. . . ."

Frankie gave the guy the sort of brain-piercing

look she usually reserves for me when I act like a total doofus. "Define *someplace!*" she snarled.

His face showed fear, then suddenly cleared. "I remember now! He was going to find an apothecary."

"Is that the camel with one hump or two?" I asked. "And why would he want a camel anyway?"

Everyone looked at me like I was the doofus again.

"Never mind," I whispered.

"An apothecary is not a camel," the man said. "He is a maker of medicines and potions—"

Frankie gasped. "Medicines and potions and— poisons! Devin, you know Romeo. If he's all bent out of shape thinking Juliet's dead, he might want to, you know, keep her company—"

"In other words, make himself dead, too?"

"Exactly. He might take poison. You know those kids. They're way into overdoing it. Remember Juliet and that dagger she pulled out at Friar Laurence's place?"

I nodded. "Yeah."

We pondered that as we took off in search of an apothecary shop.

The first four places we found were closed. The sign over the fifth one was old and peeling, but it told us that it was the one we wanted. The sign was in English.

"A dead giveaway," I said. "The lingo of Shakespeare."

We raced up to the door. The place was awesomely seedy. There was a dead turtle hanging in the grimy window, a stuffed alligator on the counter, dusty bottles and rusted boxes all over the floor. The place stank something awful, too. It was like a combo smell of a garbage can and the sharp sting of a doctor's office, mixed with after-game locker room. Not my favorite smells.

We pushed our way in and found sitting behind a counter what must have been the thinnest man alive.

"Um, excuse me, sir," I said. "Did a guy come in here looking really sad?"

The man grinned, showing a bunch of teeth not there. "Fellow by the name of Romeo?"

"That's him!" said Frankie. "What did he want?"

"He asked for two things," the man said, coughing slightly. "But I told him it's against the law for me to sell him the first thing he wanted."

I gulped loudly. "What did he want . . . exactly?"

"Poison—"

"I knew it!" yelped Frankie. "Romeo wanted poison! I hope you didn't give it to him—"

"Of course, I didn't give it to him!" said the man.

"Great!" I said.

"I *sold* it to him."

"Oh, no!" we gasped.

"Strong stuff, it is, too," the old man said. "Even if you had the strength of twenty men, it would strike you down in an instant."

"Yikes!" I cried. "We're too late!"

"Maybe not," said the man. "I just remembered what the second thing he asked for was. But I didn't have one anyway. So he's probably still looking for it. . . ."

"Well?" said Frankie. "What was it?"

"An iron bar," said the man.

"An iron bar?" I said. "What does he want an iron bar for? Is he changing tires?"

The old man did what I think was a shrug of his bony old shoulders. "He said he had to move a heavy door."

Frankie jumped. "Devin! The tomb! Romeo wants to open the door to Juliet's tomb! To die with her!"

The guy opened his mouth slowly to say something else slowwwwwly, but we weren't there to hear it.

We were busy flipping the pages of the book— *kkkk!*—and on our way back to Verona.

Before it was too late!

# Chapter 17

It was nearly nighttime when we got tossed back to the next scene in Verona. We tumbled down just outside the city walls, not far from Friar Laurence's hut.

We peeked inside, but he was gone.

"Looks like he left in a hurry," said Frankie. "His stew is only half eaten."

"That doesn't mean anything," I said. "Have you actually smelled that stew. I mean . . . uck! What does he put in there—"

"Devin? Focus?" said Frankie.

"Right. Sorry. Okay, let's see. He probably found out that Romeo never got the letter he sent. Which means that Romeo is on his way to the tomb to use the poison he got. Oh man, it's all happening too fast. Frankie, we're losing it!"

"I'm not giving up!" she said. "Let's go!"

We flashed out of there and went straight for the Verona city graveyard. I imagined that even in the full sunlight, it was a spooky place. But now, with night falling on the tombs, and every sound seeming to be the noise of some spooky creature, it was truly frightening.

Finally, we came to a small square house built of shiny red stone. At the top of a shallow set of wide stairs, was a black iron door set between two columns. Above the door the name CAPULET was carved into the stone.

"Whoa, do you think . . . Juliet's in there?" I said.

Frankie nodded, her frown growing deeper and deeper by the minute. "Not a nice place to sleep."

"None of this place is nice," I said, looking around at all the other vaults and gravestones, some with weeping angels carved on them. "If I have my way, there will be two less dead folks in this story."

"You mean you and me, right?" asked Frankie.

"Then four," I said. "I meant Romeo and Juliet."

Suddenly, a low moaning sound came from up ahead.

We dived behind a small hedge of bushes lining the path to the tomb.

"A ghost!" I gasped. "A ghost? I knew it—"

"Will you shhh?" Frankie hissed, peeking out through the leaves. "It's not a ghost. It's Paris. And a boy. The boy's carrying a bunch of flowers."

I looked. "Okay, he's not a ghost. And the flowers make sense. Paris was supposed to marry her."

We watched Paris walk quietly up to Capulet vault.

"Give me thy torch, boy," he said. "And hide here. The night watch is on patrol tonight, for fear of some new trouble between the Montagues and Capulets. If you see anyone, whistle then to me. I want to put these blossoms on Juliet's grave."

The boy gave Paris the bunch of flowers and scurried off into the shadows on the far side of the tomb. Paris stepped up to the cold carved stone of the vault.

He knelt before the door. "Juliet, sweet flower, with flowers I decorate your resting place, and water them with my tears. Every night shall I do this for you—"

*Eeeeoooeee!* The boy whistled loudly.

Paris jumped to his feet. "Something doth approach!" He ducked around to the back of the tomb.

"Frankie, I'm scared," I said.

"You and me both," she said.

As we crouched behind the bushes, another figure approached. We knew right away who it was, and why he was there.

"Romeo!" said Frankie. "Psst! Watch out!"

I shook my head. "He can't hear us. We'd better get closer, without the guards seeing us."

The night watch was everywhere, marching

around between the tombs. I could see their torches blazing red against the black night. We couldn't shout at Romeo, in case the guards heard and went after him. And maybe us.

Romeo looked both ways and then pulled out a long, metal rod. It was the iron bar that the apothecary said Romeo was looking for. He set it under the door, and after lots of groaning and grunting, and bending and lifting, the iron door ground its way across the surface of the stone.

"Open, jaws of death!" said Romeo as he beheld the darkness within. "I'll cram thee with more food—"

Frankie gasped. "He means himself!"

Paris crept around the side of the tomb. "What?" he said. "This is that banished, haughty Montague, that murdered my love's cousin. He is come to do some villainous shame to the dead bodies!"

Paris leaped up from around the vault, pulling out his sword. "Condemned villain, I do apprehend thee! Obey and go with me, for thou must die."

Romeo turned to him, his face visible for the first time in Paris's torchlight. It showed how pale and thin he had become. But his eyes had a strange sort of fire in them.

"Paris," he said. "Good gentle youth, tempt not a desperate man. By heaven, I love thee better than myself, for I come hither armed against myself—"

"Put down that torch and take up thy sword," said Paris.

Frankie screamed as Paris jumped at Romeo, his sword drawn. Romeo dodged the swinging blade, sending Paris stumbling forward.

"A fight?" said Romeo, his eyes blazing. "Then you shall have a fight!" He tossed down the torch and tugged out his blade and the two young men went at it.

*Clang! Clank! Swit! Plink!*

They clashed swords all up and down the front steps of the tomb, the sound of steel against steel echoing across the graveyard.

"It's going to bring the night watch!" I said.

"We have to stop this!" Frankie said, jumping up. "Romeo, Paris—stop!"

"What?" said Romeo. Paris took the opportunity to lunge suddenly, but Romeo twisted aside, his sword flying up and out of the way.

Almost.

Paris stopped suddenly. "I am slain! Oh, I am slain!"

"No!" said Frankie, stopping, too. "Oh, no!"

"Romeo," Paris groaned, "Romeo, if thou be merciful, lay me in the tomb next to my Juliet. . . ."

Romeo knelt down to lift him up. "In faith . . . I will. Oh, Paris, why did it come to this?" He carried him in.

"We have to tell him before it's too late," I said.

"Maybe it already is," she said, holding the book

up. "Maybe we can't change it. It's like a train wreck happening in slow motion. It's going to happen. I know it is. Our happy ending is crumbling right before our eyes!"

I looked at her. Then I shook my head. "No, I won't believe it, Frankie. You and me. We can change things. We can make them good. I know we can. Come on. Come on!"

I pulled her with me into the darkness of the tomb. Romeo had laid Paris down next to Juliet's tomb. Then, holding a candle up to Juliet, he looked at her closely.

"Romeo!" I said. "She's alive. She's alive."

"Believe us," said Frankie. "She's just sleeping."

I suddenly had an idea. It was a gamble, a severe gamble, but it just might work. Romeo had a crazy look in his eyes that was all about not listening to people. I had to try to reach him.

"Romeo," I said, "we know Juliet's alive . . ."

"Devin," said Frankie, "are you sure—"

"We know it . . . because . . . take a look at this!"

I yanked off my tunic and tossed it out the door. Romeo was left staring at my funky Shakespeare T-shirt.

"This is the guy who wrote the story you're in," I said. "That's right, a story by a guy named Shakespeare! Frankie and I are reading it. Friar Laurence gave Juliet a sleeping potion. It's all part of the story. In another few minutes—she'll wake up—"

"It's true," said Frankie, pulling her dress up over her T-shirt and shorts and flinging it to the floor. "Listen to Devin. Juliet is alive!"

Romeo's forehead just about wrinkled up into the biggest single wrinkle ever known to man.

It was cruel to do what we did, but it was our only hope. Maybe we couldn't change the play, but we could stop it cold.

Only we couldn't.

Taking off our costumes was the biggest mistake ever.

We could tell just by looking at Romeo, that the instant we were out of costume, we were suddenly out of the play. We were no more than two people in the audience. It was as if Romeo could no longer see or hear us.

"Romeo, listen!" I said.

"Romeo!" said Frankie.

It was no use. It was like shouting at a movie screen.

Slowly, he moved over to Juliet. She lay silent and unmoving on a slab of cold marble surrounded by candles, still dressed in her white wedding dress.

Nearby was another stone, with Tybalt laying on that.

Romeo slid his hand into a pocket and pulled out a small bottle of dark liquid. "Oh, my love, my wife. Death that hath taken thy breath, hath had no power yet upon thy beauty—"

"Because she's not dead!" I shouted.

"—in thy lips, and in thy cheeks, Death's pale flag is not advanced there—"

Frankie started to cry. "There's a reason for that!"

Not hearing a word, Romeo opened the bottle and raised it to his lips. "Here will I remain," he said. "Oh, here will I set up my everlasting rest. Eyes, look your last. Arms, take your last embrace. . . ."

He drank the liquid, then shuddered. "Oh, true apothecary, thy drugs are quick! Thus with a kiss . . . I die."

And he fell. He slumped to the ground next to Juliet's tomb, his hand still clasped in hers.

"Oh, man!" Frankie wailed. "This is too sad! And we couldn't do a thing! We couldn't do a stupid thing!"

There was a sudden voice calling from outside.

"If it's the prince's guards," I said, "we'll never be able to explain this. Let's hide—"

We dashed behind Juliet's stone, scrambled back into our costumes, and crouched there, watching helplessly, in the flickering candlelight, as life quickly left poor Romeo.

# Chapter 18

The voice called out again.

But we realized it wasn't the guard's voice. It was Friar Laurence's. He clambered breathlessly up the steps just as we finished putting our costumes back on.

"Saint Francis, be my speed! Fear comes upon me. I fear some terrible thing has happened. But . . . who's there?"

We crept out from behind the slab.

"Just us," I said. "And a whole lot of dead folks."

The friar's face fell nearly to the floor. He blinked in the candlelight. "Romeo? Romeo! Is it your blood that stains the stony entrance to this tomb? Oh, so pale you are! And who is this? Paris? Ohhhh!"

Juliet stirred on the slab, turned a little, then sat up.

She looked around. "Dear Devin, Frankie, Friar, where is my Romeo?"

*Clank!*

"The watch!" said Friar Laurence. "Juliet, come away from here. Thy husband, Romeo . . . lies dead. And Paris, too. Come, my dear. I will take you to a sisterhood of holy nuns, and we shall—"

More voices shouted outside.

"Wait," Juliet whispered. "My Romeo . . . dead?"

"Do not stay to question," said the friar. "The watch is coming. I dare no longer stay!"

With that, the friar darted through the front door of the vault and out into the darkness beyond. But Juliet didn't move. She saw Romeo on the floor and stared at him as if she didn't believe what she was seeing.

Then she spotted something in his hand. She slid to the floor next to him. "What's this? A vial closed up in my true love's hand?"

"It's poison," I said. "He thought you were dead. We couldn't stop him. But at least you're okay. Now, come on. We really don't want the guards to catch us here. The prince is way mad already—"

A voice shouted, "What noise comes from there?"

I tried to pull Juliet up. "We need to leave—"

Frankie peeked out the door. "There's still a chance, but the guards are closing in!"

"Then I'll be brief," said Juliet. "Oh, happy dagger, take me to my love. Romeo—let me die with you!"

"Dagger?" I said.

"What?" said Frankie. "Where did she get that! No!"

But it was too late. We rushed to stop her, but Juliet pushed us away. There was a sudden flash of silver in the candlelight, a sigh, and Juliet slumped next to her Romeo.

"Juliet!" Frankie screamed.

But it was clear that the girl was already gone. She'd said her last line, and it wasn't a good one.

Footsteps were right outside. "The ground is bloody," someone said. "Search the churchyard!"

Frankie and I crouched down on the floor of the tomb.

Everyone rushed in.

The leader of the watch stood aghast at the sight. "Pitiful sight," he muttered. "Paris slain, Juliet newly dead who was put here two days ago. You there!" he said to a guard. "Go tell the prince. Run to the Capulets. Rouse the sleeping Montagues to see this tragedy."

I glanced at Frankie. She looked at me.

Yeah. It was a tragedy, all right.

And we couldn't stop it or change it.

In a few minutes, it was like a sad reunion of all

the characters still alive, crowding around all the ones who weren't.

The prince himself entered, lighting the place with a blazing torch. "What terrible occurrence calls us from our rest?"

Mr. Capulet hustled up and pushed away the guards. His wife came stumbling right behind him.

"People in the street cry Romeo," Mrs. Capulet said. "Some Juliet, and some Paris—and all run to our family tomb!"

She staggered into the tomb. A moment later, she cried a muffled cry.

Montague forced his way in next. "My wife," he said, "my wife . . . is dead tonight. Grief over my son's banishment broke her heart and stopped her breath. What tragedy is here? What happened, tell me!"

Friar Laurence gave the crowd a whole summary of what had happened. Frankie and I broke down a couple of times—so did everyone else—because the story was so sad, but, strangely, it actually felt good to get it all out.

When the friar was finishing up, I raised my hand.

"I just wanted to say that everybody, the friar, me, Frankie, Benvolio, everybody tried to stop all these folks from dying. But we just . . . couldn't. . . ."

"It's true," said Frankie, wiping her face and taking over when I got too choked up. "We wanted a happy ending to the story. We tried lots of stuff, but we just couldn't change it. The only way the ending could have been changed is if . . . if . . ."

"Yes?" said the prince. "If what?"

I knew what Frankie meant, and I took over. "If the Montagues and Capulets had gotten over their problems with one another. This here, all these nice dead people, is what happens when fighting becomes more important than family."

We were done. We went quiet. So did everybody else. But I could tell from the expression on his face that the prince agreed with us. It was a cool feeling. If he were a teacher, he'd probably have given us an A.

"Listen to these children," he said, finally. "Even though they are young, they have seen the truth of what tragedy has happened here."

Frankie nudged me. "I think he thinks we did okay."

The prince went on. "Capulet, Montague—see what a punishment is laid upon your hate? Romeo dead. Juliet dead! And all are punished."

Capulet hung his head. "Oh, brother Montague, give me thy hand. My Juliet is gone."

"But not forgotten," said Montague, clasping his former enemy's hand. "For I will raise her statue in pure gold. Forever will Verona know of true and faithful Juliet."

"And Romeo's statue shall be joined to hers," said Capulet. "And never be forgotten."

There seemed nothing more to say. The prince stepped forward in the quiet and began to speak. Frankie showed me the page and I read along.

*"A glooming peace this morning with it brings,*
*The sun for sorrow will not show his head.*
*Go hence to have more talk of these sad things.*
*Some shall be pardoned and some punished:*
*For never was a story of more woe*
*Than this of Juliet and her Romeo."*

No one said anything for a while. Suddenly, Frankie nudged me. "That was it, Dev. The last line."

I shivered. It was really over. And to make sure of it, a sudden bright blue light sizzled just outside the tomb.

"The zapper gates!" I whispered.

"Time to go," she said. "And like Juliet said back when a happy ending still seemed possible, 'parting is such sweet sorrow. . . .'"

With that, Frankie and I slipped quietly out of the tomb, dashed down the steps, and launched ourselves right into the sizzling blue light of the zapper gates.

# Chapter 19

*Kkkkkk!*

We tumbled and jumbled and nearly crumbled apart, but were finally hurled into the library workroom—*floop! flooop!*—at the very moment Mr. Wexler and Mrs. Figglehopper burst in.

"Aha!" said our teacher, giving us the wiggly eyebrow treatment. "I see you found the costumes."

Mrs. Figglehopper laughed to see us sprawled on the floor. "But I never thought you'd actually try them on."

Frankie grinned. "I guess we're really into our parts."

"And I'm really into these tights!" I said, beginning to squirm. "So into them, I can hardly get out!"

"I think we'd all better get to the cafeteria," Mr.

Wexler said, opening the doors for us. "As soon as we're ready, we can begin our play. Too bad you didn't have a chance to read it."

Frankie and I smiled at each other as we hustled down the hallway.

"Oh, I think we get the basic story—" I said.

"—of Juliet and her Romeo," said Frankie, giving me a wink. "And I am definitely playing Juliet."

"I think I could play Romeo pretty good, too," I said.

"Oh?" said Mrs. Figglehopper. "And what changed your mind about being in the play?"

I wasn't sure how to answer that. But then I remembered what she had told us earlier. "Hey, a good story is a good story!"

Well, to make a good story short, our class put on the play for the rest of the school, and everyone flipped out.

They laughed at the funny parts and cried at the end. Frankie and I did our best to make it a fun play, but, hey, a tragedy is a tragedy.

We had excellent death scenes. I staggered all over the place before I plopped on the stage. Frankie made all kinds of wailing noises, then slumped over in a heap.

The best part was popping up at the end to take our bows.

After it was all over, Mr. Wexler applauded probably louder than everybody. Frankie and I had a feeling that, like the prince of Verona, he thought we did okay.

That meant a lot.

"Frankie, it's funny," I said, as we put away our costumes. "Both of us tried really hard to change the sad ending to a happy one. But even though we couldn't, even though it's a real bummer of a story, I still sort of feel okay about it."

She nodded. "I know exactly what you mean. It's like what the prince said. 'Go hence to have more talk of these sad things.' You do want to talk about it. It makes you feel better by talking about the whole tragedy of it."

"Because you get to talk it over with your pals."

We headed through the halls to our classroom.

"Plus," I said, "we can also make sure the bad things don't happen again. That's what a tragedy is good for."

Frankie nodded thoughtfully. "Nicely said, Devin. And you know what else is a tragedy?"

"What?"

"Your legs . . . in tights."

I gave her a look, then burst out laughing. "You looked pretty funny in that big grape-colored dress, you know!"

"Oh, yeah? Well, thou hast knobby knees!"

"And thou lookest funny climbing a rope ladder!"

"Soft, what doofus in yonder desk sits!"

"Uh-oh, Frankie," I said. "We better call the nurse right away. I think we're coming down with a bad case of . . . of . . ."

"What?"

"Shakespeare!"

Dear Reader:

Alas and forsooth! As Frankie and Devin discovered, poor Juliet and her Romeo do come to a sad end. Yet from the first performance of this play in 1595, the world seems to have taken the story of these two "star-crossed" lovers straight to its heart. I know I have. And I think Frankie and Devin have, too.

Shakespeare! A mere mention of his name conjures a list of the finest plays ever composed: *Hamlet, King Lear, A Midsummer Night's Dream, Macbeth, As You Like It, Othello, Twelfth Night.*

But who was William Shakespeare?

In fact, not much is known about him. We do know that he was born in 1564, probably on April 23, in the small English country town of Stratford-upon-Avon. He married Anne Hathaway when he was eighteen, and together they had three children. Sometime later, William left Stratford for the great city of London.

By 1594 he had formed his own theatrical group, The Lord Chamberlain's Men. Within a few short years he began to be acclaimed as a writer of hilarious comedies and noble tragedies. By all accounts, William was a fast writer, too, penning two or more plays a year (and probably acting in every single one of them!).

In 1599, the famous Globe Theater was built on the banks of the Thames river in London, with William as one of its joint owners. The Globe was a large, eight-sided, open-air theater with a stage jutting out into the middle, where the crowd stood. From the time it was built, most of William's plays premiered there.

The last major play he wrote was *The Tempest*, about a powerful, but aging magician who gives up his power in order to live as a normal person again. It was first performed in 1611. That year, William himself seems to have retired from the London scene, to live his remaining years in Stratford as a country gentleman.

Shakespeare died on his birthday, April 23, 1616, and is buried in the same church where he was baptized. Stratford-upon-Avon is now a world-famous tourist attraction.

*Romeo and Juliet* is certainly one of Shakespeare's most famous plays, but did you know that Romeo and Juliet were the names of two real people who actually lived (and, yes, died) in Verona, Italy, in the 14th century? Well, it's true. Of course, what William made of that story is full of beautiful poetry, swift action, boisterous humor, and tearful tragedy. It's no secret why people proclaim his plays the greatest in the English language!

Speaking of secrets, I'd better go turn off those pesky zapper gates. I don't want anyone to discover my secret!

Until then, see you where the books are!

I. M. Figglehopper